"Who are you?"

"Look at me."

She did. Familiarity flashed, but no name came with it. "Who are you?"

He blanched. "I'm Toby, Robin. Toby Potter."

"I...I'm scared. Why am I scared?" Tremors shook her, and Toby's look of concern deepened.

"Someone tried to kill you," he said.

She blinked. "Who?"

"I don't know. I was hoping you could tell me."

Robin raised a hand to her head. "I...can't think. Everything's a jumble. Why can't I remember? You're acting like I should know you. But I don't!" Panic clawed at her.

His warm hands gripped hers. "It's okay. Sh..." He pulled her to him and for some reason she let him. She needed to believe him. "Give it some time, and it'll all come back to you. But for now, let's head to the hospital. You ready?"

"I'm ready." Ready for what, she wasn't exactly sure, but Toby seemed to know what he was doing. And for now, that was going to have to be enough.

Lynette Eason is a bestselling, award-winning author who makes her home in South Carolina with her husband and two teenage children. She enjoys traveling, spending time with her family and teaching at various writing conferences around the country. She is a member of Romance Writers of America and American Christian Fiction Writers. Lynette can often be found online interacting with her readers. You can find her at Facebook.com/lynette.eason and on Twitter, @lynetteeason.

Books by Lynette Eason

Love Inspired Suspense

Wrangler's Corner

The Lawman Returns
Rodeo Rescuer
Protecting Her Daughter
Classified Christmas Mission
Christmas Ranch Rescue
Vanished in the Night
Holiday Amnesia

Military K-9 Unit

Explosive Force

Family Reunions

Hide and Seek
Christmas Cover-Up
Her Stolen Past

Rose Mountain Refuge

Agent Undercover
Holiday Hideout
Danger on the Mountain

Visit the Author Profile page at Harlequin.com for more titles.

HOLIDAY AMNESIA

LYNETTE EASON

HARLEQUIN® LOVE INSPIRED® SUSPENSE

LOVE INSPIRED BOOKS

Recycling programs for this product may not exist in your area.

ISBN-13: 978-1-335-49077-3

Holiday Amnesia

Copyright © 2018 by Lynette Eason

www.Harlequin.com

Printed in U.S.A.

According to thy mercy remember thou me
for thy goodness' sake, O Lord.
—Psalms 25:7

To all of the readers who buy my books.
I appreciate you so much!

ONE

Dr. Robin Hardy looked up from her microscope and frowned when the voices reached her over the Christmas music she had playing softly through the one earbud she wore. She never wore two when working just in case someone needed her attention. A habit she'd developed after being scared out of her skin by coworkers tapping her on the shoulder.

Some people played only music. She liked the radio app and the commentary that came with it. And she'd hoped the cheery tunes and upbeat voices would lighten the heaviness in her heart.

So far it hadn't worked.

A part-time professor at the Middle Tennessee State University, she spent the majority of her time teaching virology research to eager young minds.

The rest of the time—too much time, some might say—she worked in the lab along with several other scientists. None of whom were on the schedule to be here tonight. She'd come because she'd craved something to take her mind off the fact that she'd been betrayed by someone she'd considered a good friend. With the potential to be something more.

Hurt feelings and righteous anger didn't promote restful nights. So, she worked. And fumed. And vowed never to trust another charming, good-looking, smooth-talking male again.

Toby Potter, with his dancing eyes, finger-magnet five o'clock shadow and perpetually mussed caramel-colored hair, had used her. The rat. Pretending he cared when the whole time he was just getting close to her so he could get close to her research and have firsthand knowledge of what was going on in the lab. And while she just wanted to be mad, tears once again blurred her vision.

Stop thinking about him.

Easier said than done. It was hard to turn off the hurt. She blinked and sniffed—and tried to focus. The voices grew louder. Unable to hear more than the fact someone else was in the lab, she supposed a couple of fellow scientists had decided to put in a few more hours just like her.

But they probably weren't using work to distract them—to keep their minds off of people better just forgotten. Unfortunately, work wasn't doing anything to help her forget.

She studied the specimen, trying to see it through her tears. And finally gave up. She'd thought Toby was different, that his interest in her work was because he was interested in *her*. Boy, was she a lousy judge of character.

Heated words snapped her head around. "What in the world?" she muttered.

Curious, she removed the slide from the scope and returned it to its secure slot in the box next to her. She slipped off the gloves and tossed them into the hazardous waste bin. Most of the lights had been turned off and she usually liked it that way, but right now, they held a foreboding that crept over her. The farther she walked from her workstation, the darker it got, the blackness like a glove closing around her.

She shivered.

Then laughed at herself, mentally reviewing the security in the lab. No one without authorization could get in. And no one with authorization was anyone to be afraid of. While the university lab wasn't a Level 4 secure lab working with deadly pathogens, Robin still considered her research and teaching an important part of the process for training upcoming scientists. And it was very secure.

Light returned. Someone else was working at the far end of the large building in a corner station. Or *had been* working. Possibly. Right now, the two men standing face-to-face looked like they were ready to start throwing punches.

"The bidding has already started. I need that virus now!"

"It's not ready. I told you. I'm still working out some issues, but I should have it soon."

Their words echoed through the large area.

Virus? Bidding? She didn't recognize the first voice, but the second one belonged to Alan Roberts—a virologist like her.

"How soon is soon?" the first voice asked.

"Soon! Okay? I'll call when I'm ready." A pause. "I'm serious. I think I've got it, I just need to run a couple of more tests and then it'll be ready."

"How much longer?"

"Twelve hours, okay?" Alan threw the notebook onto his workstation area and it landed on top of the manila file folders that always seemed to overflow his desk. "I have to make sure it's right. The first test said it was."

"Then why more tests?"

"To make sure. If you sell a defective product, your investors might take exception. Just let me do my job, then you can do yours."

"Twelve hours. That's it. I'll let the buyer know we're a go."

"Fine," Alan said. "You have my account number. Make sure the money lands there like it's supposed to."

"Of course."

Robin eased closer, careful not to do anything stupid like knock something over or misstep. She could see the two men huddled in the corner. She and Alan shared a love of the classics, and he usually had a jovial personality in spite of his daughter's medical bills. Leukemia had taken its toll on the family.

A deep scowl creased his lean face. "I'll figure it out. Get out of here before someone sees you."

"Right."

Robin held her breath as the second man turned on his heel and strode to the door that would lead him out of the back of the lab. How had he even gotten in? He'd need a key card to get out. The sick feeling that had been growing as she listened now blossomed into full-fledged nausea.

They were selling a virus? But what kind? And how would they get access to it? Or had they *built* it?

Alan slammed a fist on the desk and closed his eyes for a brief moment. Unsure whether to leave or confront him, she hesitated. A shot sounded, and Alan jerked, then dropped to the floor. Robin clapped a hand over her mouth.

Blood from the bullet wound in the middle of his back stained his white lab coat. Robin swallowed a sob, terror pounding through her. Alan rolled with a grunt. Another pop stilled him. The killer ran out the door. She heard two more gunshots as she turned to run. But she had to check on Alan. She hurried to his side and knelt next to him. His eyes were open with his pupils fixed.

Robin scrambled to her feet, her lungs desperate for air, adrenaline racing. The door opened and Alan's killer stood there, hand grasping the collar of the man Alan had been speaking with. He dragged him back into the lab, then released his hold. In slow motion, she watched the victim thud to the floor.

Time sped up again when the killer swept a hand over Alan's desk, raking up the files he'd been working through. Vaguely, her mind registered that the shooter had been in the lab the whole time. He'd heard the same conversation she had. And he'd had a gun. Why?

Frozen, she ordered herself to move and couldn't. The man turned and jerked when he saw her standing there. Hard eyes never left hers. Breath caught in her constricted throat. "You killed them," she whispered. "Why? How could you?"

"Call it an unexpected moneymaking opportunity that I'd be crazy to pass up." He lifted his phone. "I've hit a small snag in the plan. Warn me if anyone approaches while I take care of this."

"Snag in what plan?" Why wasn't she running? Run!

"Sorry, Robin." He lifted his weapon.

Robin screamed and lunged sideways. The bullet shattered the beaker on the table behind her. Stumbling, refusing to fall, she got her feet under her and raced through the lab, dodging chairs and tables, her goal the back hallway that held the break room, conference room and restrooms. She'd never make it to the exit.

Another shot whizzed too close to her cheek as the footsteps behind her pounded faster. *No!* She would *not* die like this. She burst into the men's bathroom, slammed the door and locked it. If he saw her dart down the hallway, he'd assume she'd go into the women's bathroom. Locking herself in the men's might buy her an extra lifesaving minute or two.

She shoved her hand into her lab coat pocket and froze. Her phone. Where was it?

A picture of it sitting on her workstation flashed through her mind. With no way to call for help, her panic bloomed, exploding through her.

Think. Think.

Panting, lungs straining for air, she went to the window.

A loud boom shuddered through the building and sent her to her knees. The door exploded inward and slammed into her like a missile, knocking her to the floor face-first. Her forehead connected with the solid tile floor. Pain arched through her and blackness coated her.

Toby Potter watched the flames shoot toward the sky as he raced toward the building. "Robin!"

Sirens screamed closer. Toby had been on his way home when he'd spotted Robin's car in the parking lot of the lab. Ever since Robin had discovered his deception—orders to get close to her and figure out what was going on in the lab—she'd kept him at arm's length, her narrow-eyed stare hot enough to singe his eyebrows if he dare try to get too close.

Tonight, he'd planned to apologize profusely—again—and ask if there was anything he could do to earn her trust back. Only to pull into the parking lot, be greeted by the loud boom and watch flames shoot out of the window near the front door.

Heart pounding, Toby scanned the front door and rushed forward only to be forced back by the intense heat. Smoke billowed toward the dark night sky while the fire grew hotter and bigger. Mini-explosions followed. Chemicals.

"Robin!"

Toby jumped into his truck and drove around to the

back only to find it not much better although it did seem to be more smoke than flames. The thick cloud decreased his visual field, but he had to try. Robin was in that building, and he was afraid he'd failed to protect her. Big time.

The lab backed up to a wooded area left by the designers of the campus to make it feel less city and more rural. He'd always appreciated the beauty of the place, and now he had visions of it burning, the trees and animals caught in the path of the flames. And Robin.

Toby parked near the tree line in case more explosions were coming. The lot on this side was smaller, just one row along the length of the building.

At the back door, he grasped the handle and pulled. Locked. Of course. Using both fists, he pounded on the glass and metal door. "Robin!"

He fumbled for the key card FBI special agent Ben Little had provided when Toby had agreed to take the case, allowing him access to the building when it would be empty. Better for snooping and spying.

Another explosion from inside rocked Toby back, but he was able to keep his feet under him. He figured the blast was on the other end of the building—where he knew Robin's station was. If she was anywhere near that station, there was no way she was still alive. "No, please no," he whispered. No one was around to hear him, but maybe God was listening.

He raced down the side of the building, trying each door only to find them locked. He wasn't getting inside. And no one was coming out. Where were the fire trucks? He knew his concept of time was skewed. What was merely seconds seemed like hours.

Heart in his throat, he finally backed away, his mind flashing through times spent with Robin. Eating at the university cafeteria, walks around the small pond near the library, laughter at the old movies in the campus theater. Her fury when she discovered his duplicity. He blinked and shook his head.

Initially, his assignment had been to get close to her and find out what was going on in the lab. Over the past month, he'd found himself wanting to know *her*, convinced she wasn't involved in anything suspect but that she might have information she didn't know she had. Now, he'd failed her.

Grief gripped him. This wasn't supposed to happen. He'd quit the CIA because he was tired of the covert life. He'd been working as a professor at the university—and healing from life's wounds—when his former handler and friend, turned FBI agent, had roped him into helping with his case.

Toby grabbed his phone from his pocket and punched in the number for Ben Little. It rang twice as a fire truck finally screamed around the side of the building. "Yeah?"

"Ben, it's me. Someone blew up the lab and I think Robin's inside."

"What!"

"I failed her, Ben." He didn't recognize his own voice. "I failed." Again. Another woman had died because of him.

Robin blinked. Then coughed. Her head pounded in time with her heart. The pain nearly sent her back into the black abyss, but she drew in a smoky breath and shoved herself up off the bathroom floor. Darkness swirled, and spots danced before her eyes while sweat rolled down her temples and between her shoulder blades. Nausea doubled her over, but she stumbled to the door and touched the handle.

Only to jerk back when it burned her hand. Fighting

to stay upright and conscious, she staggered to the window and unlocked it. Then realized it was sealed shut. The double-paned frosted window that ran from ceiling to floor was simply for looks, not for opening.

Groaning, she looked around for something, anything to break the glass. An idea sparked in her smoke-fogged brain and she stumbled to the nearest stall. Grabbing the top of the ceramic tank, she hefted it with a grunt and carried it back to the window, ignoring her churning stomach, pounding head and shaky legs. She gathered her strength and heaved it against the glass. Once. Twice. A large crack formed in the window. Her legs gave out and she fell, gasping, choking, her lungs grabbing at any remaining oxygen in the room.

Get up! You're going to die if you don't!

Pulling on the last of her strength, Robin hauled herself and the tank lid up. "Ahhh!" She slammed it against the glass.

The window shattered, the pieces falling to the ground outside. "Oh, thank you," she breathed.

She shrugged out of her lab coat, placed it over the jagged edges and hauled herself through the opening. She fell to the ground on top of the glass. Her palms stung and she flinched but pushed to her feet, coughing and gagging.

Robin staggered away from the burning building, blinded by the smoke and desperate for clean air. The sirens and red flashing lights registered. She pressed a bleeding hand to her pounding head and finally found herself at the edge of the parking lot. She staggered into the trees and retched.

The world continued to spin, and she fell to the ground, her cheek pressing into the pine needles. She had to run.

But why?

She should know why but couldn't bring the reason into focus.

Oh, because of him.

He'd tried to kill her.

His eyes closed. Then opened. Her head continued its hammering and her ears rang with an annoying high-pitched frequency.

Rolling onto her back, she stared up at the swirling trees while she tried to figure out what had happened. There'd been an explosion. Something had hit her, and she'd fallen.

Voices reached her. Instinctively, she scrambled to her knees and crawled behind the nearest tree while she made out the words "…find her. Get rid of her."

"There's no way she survived that," another voice said. "You barely got out alive and she was still in the building when it exploded."

"Maybe."

"No maybe about it. You said she ran into the bathroom just before the first explosion went off. She's dead."

"Make sure!"

"Fine, I'll make sure."

They had to be talking about her. Tremors set in. Shock? She curled her arms around her knees and pressed her aching forehead against them. They wanted her dead? Who? Why? No, she'd seen him. In the lab. His face blurred, and she was sick again. When her stomach calmed down, the world still spun while she tried to force her mind to work.

She had to leave. To run. She stood, using the tree to help pull herself to her feet, ignoring the pain in her hands.

As she stepped in the opposite direction of the men who wanted to kill her, a hand slapped over her mouth and pulled her back to the ground.

TWO

When Robin went limp in his arms, Toby lowered her to the ground and watched the two men stomp away from their meeting spot.

He'd been bolting back to his truck, mind whirling, grief slashing his heart to shreds, when he'd heard a loud crash behind him. He'd spun to see a figure emerge from the broken window and stagger across the parking lot and into the trees. The smoke had kept him from seeing clearly, but he'd followed, praying it was Robin but willing to help whoever it was.

He'd been almost upon her when he'd heard the faint voices but couldn't hear their words or see their faces. The fact that they seemed to be hiding, whispering and unconcerned about the burning building behind them, triggered his internal alarms.

Since the person who'd escaped the building was staying hidden and quiet, he'd done the same just a few feet behind her. When she'd turned, he'd caught a glimpse of her silhouette and relief had pounded through him when he'd realized it was definitely Robin. But he'd stayed silent, only moving when it looked like she might inadvertently reveal her presence.

And then she'd passed out in his arms.

"…kill her. Tonight." The faint order given by one of the men he could no longer see reached his ears. He didn't recognize the voice, but now knew why he needed to act with caution.

They were trying to kill Robin?

Once the men were gone, he checked her pulse. Her eyelids fluttered but didn't open. "Robin, it's me, Toby. Can you wake up?"

No response. The gash on her forehead worried him. "Robin?"

Her lashes lifted, and he breathed a sigh of relief.

"Come on, there's an ambulance over here. Let's get your head looked at."

"No. They'll find me," she whispered.

"I'll stay with you."

"No!" She rolled her head back and forth, clearly agitated. "Can't trust…anyone. Got…to…get away…please…"

"Robin, it's okay, I promise. Just let them check your head."

But she didn't answer. She'd passed out again. He suspected she had a concussion, he just prayed it wasn't anything worse. Great. Now what?

The fact that she could move her neck without apparent trouble or pain decided for him. If she didn't want to risk being examined here at the scene, then fine. Now that he had a second chance to keep her safe, he wasn't about to fail her.

The hospital wasn't too far. He shrugged out of his heavy coat and tore the long sleeves from his T-shirt. He wrapped one around his nose and mouth, then covered her face with the other one. He lifted her into his arms and rose to his feet.

Under cover of the smoke that now blanketed the wooded area, Toby made his way back to his vehicle at the edge of the lot and loaded her into the back seat. Once he had her covered with the blanket, he climbed behind the wheel and made his way out of the parking lot.

Emergency crews were too busy putting out the blaze to bother noticing him. Law enforcement and campus security were on-site, but until they figured out the reason for the explosions, they would have no cause to stop him. He hoped.

Once they started their investigation, if there was foul play involved—and after overhearing the conversation in the woods between the two men, he was pretty sure there was—they'd watch security footage and see him leaving in his truck. And they'd want to talk to him. Which was fine, but for now, he wanted to get Robin to a safe place where she could receive the care she needed for her head wound.

Robin woke with a start and bit back a groan, swallowing the nausea that clawed at the back of her throat. She lay still while trying to get a grip on the pain that came from every part of her. She finally registered the gentle movement beneath her. The hum of the engine, the low volume of the radio. No Christmas music on this one, but someone saying something about a fire at the university lab?

She was in a vehicle—a large one since she stretched the length of the back seat without any trouble. But who was driving? And why was she sleeping in the back? And why did her entire body hurt?

Sitting up required effort so she stayed still, her pounding temples convincing her that moving would be a mistake. She forced her mind to work. Or at least she tried to. But it rebelled. She simply couldn't remember where the headache had come from.

Get rid of her.

She's dead.

The words echoed, bouncing in her brain but unable to take root and tell her what they meant.

Cold fear enveloped her and the desire to run, get away, nearly strangled her. All she could see was the back of the driver's head. Who was he? Someone who wanted her dead? Was he taking her somewhere to kill her?

Get rid of her.

She's dead.

Her head rested behind the passenger seat so when the truck slowed to a stop, she reached up, popped the door and shoved it open.

"Robin! Stop!"

No, she had to get out. In an awkward half crawl, half lunge, she managed to propel herself from the back seat onto the asphalt.

But she couldn't move fast enough. The pain was too much, the nausea overwhelming. She lost whatever she might have had left in her stomach.

Gentle hands held her head while she dry-heaved. "You have a concussion," a man said. A white tissue appeared in front of her face. She took it and wiped her mouth. Then a water bottle replaced the tissue. She took that, too. Rinsed and spit. "Who are you?" she whispered.

"Look at me."

She did. Familiarity flashed, but no name came with it. "Who are you?"

He blanched. "I'm Toby, Robin. Toby Potter." His hand went to the wound on her forehead. "We need to get you to a doctor. We're almost to the hospital."

"I… I'm scared. Why am I scared?" Tremors shook her, and Toby's look of concern deepened.

"Someone tried to kill you," he said.

Get rid of her.

She's dead.

She blinked. "Who?"

"I don't know. I was hoping you could tell me."

Robin raised a hand to her head. "I...can't think. Everything's a jumble. Why can't I remember? You're acting like I should know you. But I don't!" Panic clawed at her.

His warm hands gripped hers and she flinched. He turned them over to look at her palms. "What happened?"

She stared at the cuts. "I don't know. Why don't I know?"

"It's okay. Shh..." He pulled her to him and for some reason she let him. She needed to believe him. To believe that he wouldn't hurt her, and he was there to help her. "You've had a really traumatic experience," he said. "Give it some time and it'll all come back to you. But for now, let's continue on to the hospital."

She had no words or energy left to argue. The pain was constant, and she just wanted it to go away. If Toby was out to harm her, he could have just done it. Instead, he was loading her into the front passenger seat this time. Probably so he could catch her if she tried to nose-dive out the door again.

Once she had her seat belt on, he rounded the front of the vehicle and climbed behind the wheel. "You ready?"

"I'm ready." Ready for what, she wasn't exactly sure, but Toby seemed to know what he was doing. And for now, that was going to have to be enough.

The remainder of the drive to the hospital didn't take long and was, thankfully, uneventful. When Toby pulled into the parking lot, Robin was asleep, her head propped against the window. "Robin?"

She didn't move.

"Robin, can you walk?"

She groaned and pulled away from him.

Toby rubbed his eyes, then the back of his neck. Just

as he'd decided to simply carry her inside, his phone rang. Ben. "Yes?"

"Are you all right?" his friend asked.

"I'm at the hospital. I've got Robin with me."

"They know she's alive."

"What? How?"

"The same way I know. The broken bathroom window. It's obvious she got out."

"It could have been anyone in that bathroom." Toby sighed. "But they're going to rightly assume it was her since no one else was there at the lab." He paused. "At least I don't think so. There were two guys in the woods where we were hiding. They were talking about making sure she was dead. I'm not sure if they were actually in the lab when it exploded, but I got the impression that they weren't."

"Got it."

"And, Ben?"

"Yeah?"

"I don't remember seeing any other cars in the parking lot except Robin's, but that doesn't mean someone didn't park elsewhere and walk over. You'll need to scour the security footage from different areas on campus."

"Okay. Local police are already here. They've requested FBI presence and resources, so they made it easy for us."

"Meaning you're already looking into it."

"We have a team of local and federal agencies questioning people who were on campus at the time and near the lab. So far, no one's come up with anything useful."

"Okay. Let me think." Toby drummed the steering wheel for a moment. "First and foremost, Robin's got a head wound that needs to be checked out."

"Anything else besides the head wound?"

"Some superficial wounds to her hands. What worries me the most is the confusion and memory loss." He paused. "She doesn't know me."

"Oh no. That doesn't sound good."

"Tell me about it."

"Okay, get her checked out but don't linger. They're probably going to be checking the hospitals. I'm going to be gathering information on this end and see if I can figure out who's behind the blast. You just keep her safe."

"Got it. Bye." He gave her a gentle shake and frowned when she only blinked and closed her eyes again. He gave up and went around to the passenger side, hefted her slight form in his arms and carried her into the emergency department. With one eye behind him and one in front, he caught the attention of the triage nurse. "Got an emergency here."

She took one look at them and reacted. No doubt Robin's bloody head was quite the attention-catcher. Within seconds, the nurse had them back in a room and was examining Robin. "She'll need a CT scan and a number of other tests. You'll have to wait here."

He caught her arm and pulled her to the side. "She needs police protection. She wound up like this because someone tried to kill her tonight. I don't want to leave her."

She held his gaze for a few moments, then nodded. "Are you a cop?"

"Not exactly. I'm working with the FBI. I can give you a contact number if you need proof, but I can't leave this woman."

"No ID?"

"No. Not for this assignment."

"I see."

He had a feeling she did. After several agonizing seconds of her scrutiny, she shot him one more look and nodded. "You can go."

"Thanks."

For the next six hours, Toby stayed with Robin, never leaving her side and monitoring those who entered her room with ID checks. The kind nurse who'd shown him grace by letting him stay with Robin stepped into the room.

"How's she doing?" she asked. "Has she regained consciousness yet? Is she talking and making sense?"

"She's in and out of consciousness and not making much sense when she talks." He paused. "She grew up in foster homes and is talking about one of the families she lived with when she was around ten years old, I think. She doesn't know who I am though."

"Did she know who you were before the knock on the head?"

He shot her a tight smile. "Yes. I'm very concerned."

The nurse nodded. "You're not the only one. We'd like to keep her overnight for observation," she said. "The doctor's not comfortable releasing her yet. The fact that she's still not remembering anything that happened has him wanting to take extreme cautions and the neurologist concurs."

Toby blew out a breath. "Of course." He rubbed his chin. "What about helping her remember?"

"What do you mean?"

"You know, telling her things that she doesn't remember right now in an attempt to jar her memories loose."

"The doctor said good memories would be fine. Anything that might upset her or be a shock would be better for her to remember on her own."

"I see." Well, that could work in his favor since he definitely didn't want to tell her about their last few weeks together. Not yet at least.

"I'll be back to check on her shortly," she said after adjusting the IV line.

"Thank you," Toby said.

She left, and Toby settled into the chair next to Robin's bed. He pulled out his phone and texted Ben an update, then leaned back to close his eyes for a few minutes.

When the door opened, he blinked and straightened. His gaze went to Robin who was resting peacefully, eyes shut, lips parted slightly. A male nurse in his late thirties nodded at him and pulled a syringe from his pocket. "Good morning."

"Morning." Toby frowned. "What's that?"

"Just a little more pain medicine. Want to keep her comfortable."

"I think she's fine." Toby's gaze went to the man's name tag. And found it missing. Toby stood. "Let me see some ID please. She just had some medicine not too long ago."

"I know. I read her chart. But the doctor wanted her to have this."

"What is it?"

The man huffed and aimed the needle at the IV port. "Look, I'm just following orders, okay? If you have a problem with it, take it up with the doc."

"I will." Toby stepped forward and grabbed the man's forearm. "But you're not giving her that medicine until I do. Understood?"

Fury flashed in the man's eyes, but his lips curved in a cold smile. "Of course."

"Where's your name tag?"

"I forgot it today. Why?"

Toby yanked the syringe from the man's fingers in a smooth move and shoved him away from Robin's bed. "Who are you, and how did you know she was here?"

The man bolted for the door and Toby followed, stopping just outside the door. He couldn't go after him without leaving Robin alone. He grabbed the phone and called security, describing the incident and where the man had disappeared, then turned back to find Robin sitting up in bed, blinking at him. "What's going on?" she asked.

"We're getting out of here." He grabbed her filthy clothes from the bag on the counter. "You need to put these on."

She grimaced. "Why?"

He went to the bed and took her face in his. Gently, so as not to cause her any more pain. "Look at me." He waited for her eyes to meet his and focus. The nurse's words flipped through his mind. *Don't tell her anything stressful or shocking. It's better for her to remember on her own.* He hesitated for a brief second. "Will you trust me?"

"No. I don't know you and I'm in the hospital, and I can't remember anything. Why should I trust you?"

At the edge of hysteria in her words, he made an executive decision. "You're not safe here, understand?"

"Why?"

"Because—"

"Wait a minute." She pressed a hand to her bandaged head. "There was a fire."

"That's one way of putting it. Someone set that fire, okay? In the form of explosives. And I'm pretty sure you were supposed to die in it." She stared, unblinking. "When they discovered you survived, they sent someone to finish the job. I just chased him off. At least that's the way it looks. Whether or not any of that is true, I'm not willing to chance it. We're leaving." Her eyes followed him, but he saw no sign of recognition in their depths. "Will you trust me? Please?"

"Someone tried to kill me?" she whispered. "Here? In the hospital?"

"Yes." Had he said too much? Pressed her too hard? Done irreparable damage because he hadn't followed the nurse's orders?

"Hand me the clothes and help me into the bathroom. I'll be ready to leave in about sixty seconds."

THREE

Once they'd made it out of the hospital and she'd climbed into the passenger seat of Toby's truck, Robin leaned her head back and closed her eyes in spite of the fact adrenaline wired her. Her head wasn't pounding nearly as hard as it had been, and she figured it was the medicine that was keeping the pain under control.

When Toby hauled himself into the driver's seat, she had a momentary blip of panic. What was she doing? How did she know she could trust him? But what choice did she have?

She tried to remember what had happened that had brought her to this point, but all she could pull from her mind was the phone call offering her the job at the university lab last week. She frowned. No, that was impossible. Last week it had been hot and muggy at night. She'd just walked out of the hospital to find it chilly. "What day is it? What month?"

"It's December 5th."

"December!"

"Yes, why?"

"Because the last thing I remember is getting a phone call offering me the job at the lab. That was at the beginning of June." She swallowed the panic that threatened to consume her. "Are you telling me I've lost six months?"

"That's what it sounds like, Robin, but don't panic."

A laugh escaped her. She noted that the sound bordered on the edge of hysteria. "Don't panic? Too late."

"Come on, you heard the doctor. You've had a traumatic experience. Once everything settles down, your mind will feel less threatened and your memory will probably return."

"Probably. What if it doesn't?"

He slid his hand from the wheel to grip her fingers. "We'll figure it out, Robin. I'm here to help you, okay?"

"Why?" she whispered. "What are you to me? Why can't I remember you?"

He drove with precise movements, showing his comfort with handling the large vehicle. For some reason that helped settle her. "You said you remember being hired to work at the lab. But you don't remember anything after that?"

"No. Why?"

"Because we met about a month after you started working there."

"Oh. So, we're friends?"

"Definitely friends."

She sighed. "I'm sorry I don't remember."

"It's okay. Or it will be. We just need to get you somewhere safe until the authorities can catch whoever blew up the lab."

"I'm all for them catching them, but I want to know more than who it was."

"What do you mean?"

"I want to know who and *why.*"

"Yeah, the why would be good to know." He glanced

at her. "I'm wondering if you know the answer to both of those."

"What do you mean?"

"I mean, someone obviously wants you dead. I overheard them talking in the woods."

"The woods," she said. "We were in the woods?"

"The woods behind the lab on campus. After you got out of the building, you ran into the woods and were hiding. Which is where I found you. Anyway, there were two guys talking. I couldn't see them—or hear them very well. I just caught some snatches of conversation but definitely heard them say something about killing you. Tonight."

She rubbed her forehead and winced when she accidentally pressed too hard against her wound. "So what now?"

"We get you some clothes and whatever else you need for a couple of days of hiding out."

"Hiding out? Where?" She had nothing but questions that needed answers.

"First, a motel. Then we'll work together to find a more long-term solution to keeping you safe."

"Like what?"

"I'm working on that."

While he drove for the next thirty minutes, Robin dozed off and on. The silence was tense but not awkward. Tense only because she could tell he was thinking about their next move.

"We need to fill your pain meds," he said when she blinked awake.

She frowned. "No. I don't want them." Her head and hands hurt, but the thought of a drugged unconsciousness scared her silly.

"You will when the current ones wear off. I've had a concussion before and it hurts. It may take you a while to recover."

"But if we fill the prescription, whoever's after me will be able to track us that way, won't they?"

"It's possible. The fact that you're thinking rationally is reassuring."

"Then we shouldn't stop to fill it, right?"

"By the time they show up—assuming they manage to trace it—we'll be long gone." He pulled off at an exit advertising food and lodging. "Let's try here. It's a small town off the beaten path. I think we'll be all right here for a bit."

"Okay." Robin had already made up her mind she was going to have to trust this stranger who claimed they were friends.

"So, first, let's get food. What do you want?"

"Shouldn't you know that?" She raised a brow. "If we're friends like you say we are."

He barked a short laugh. "Okay, you're not really picky. You don't do fast food on a regular basis, but I know there's no way you're going to be willing to go inside a restaurant looking like you just survived the apocalypse."

Her jaw swung. "The apocalypse? Really?"

"Okay, you're not that bad, but am I wrong?"

She huffed. "No." His spot-on assessment greatly reassured her that he knew her. The fact that she remembered nothing about *him* wasn't nearly as comforting. It was downright terrifying.

"So, do you want a burger or chicken?"

"Burger."

Once they'd ordered and received their food at the window, he pulled into a parking spot where they dug in.

"We need to get you some clothes," he said. "How do you feel about shopping?"

"I honestly don't know if I have the energy. Besides, what do you think after that whole apocalypse comment?"

He groaned. "You're going to hold that over my head, aren't you?"

She tilted her head and thought. "Yes. I think I am."

"All right. You can give me your sizes and I can grab a few things for you."

"I don't have any money. My purse, my—" She paused. "Where do I live? All I can picture is my two-bedroom apartment in Houston, Texas."

"When you took the job at the university, they offered you an apartment across the street from the university." He paused. "We live in the same building."

"Then I suppose all of my things are there."

"Except your cell phone. You always had that with you—usually in the pocket of your lab coat."

"I...don't know."

"You weren't wearing your coat when I found you, so you probably left it in the lab."

"Then the phone's gone if the fire was as bad as you say."

He nodded. "It was. I can get you a phone. As for your purse, I don't know where that would be. Sometimes you took it to the lab with you, sometimes you left it in your car—against my advice, I will say."

She'd always left her purse in the car when she didn't feel like carrying it. "Where's my car now?"

"I had it towed to your home while I was waiting for you to get out of the CT scan."

"I need to get it then."

"No, you need to be safe."

"But it has everything in there. My wallet. I—"

"Don't worry about the money, Robin. You almost died. Let me help you. You can pay me back later if it means that much to you."

She sighed. What choice did she have? "Fine. Thank you."

"Of course. Now. What size are you?"

She gave him her information and when they were finished eating, he found a large superstore and parked. "I don't want to leave you here alone."

"I'll be all right. It's busy. People are all around."

He shook his head. "I don't like it."

"You think we were followed?"

"I don't, but I just have a bad feeling about leaving you here."

"Then I'll come with you and just endure the sidelong looks I'll be sure to get."

"I've got a better idea." He pulled out his phone and dialed a number. She leaned her aching head against the window and relished the coolness of the glass against her cheek.

"Amber? Yeah. I need a favor."

Robin closed her eyes and listened as he spoke to the person on the phone. She'd almost drifted off to sleep when he hung up. She blinked at him. "Who was that?"

"A friend who is really good at protection detail. Her name is Amber Starke... I mean, Goode. She got married a couple of years ago to Lance who's a deputy in Wrangler's Corner."

"And she's coming here?"

"She's only about thirty minutes away. I'll put you two at the motel while I come back and get your prescription and some clothes for you."

Robin had no strength to argue. She just wanted a shower, then to rest her head on a pillow and shut her eyes. In that order. Before she knew it, they were parked in front of the motel.

"I've got us connecting rooms," Toby said. "Amber will be here in just a few minutes. She'll stay with you tonight and we'll figure out what to do in the morning."

"Okay." Robin climbed out of the vehicle and winced when she shut the door. Her hands had been bandaged at the hospital, and they stung. When he opened the door to the room, she stepped inside. Two beds, a dresser that held a television, a refrigerator and a microwave. The scent of pine and new carpet hung in the air and Robin was grateful the place was clean. And nice. She went to the bed and sat.

Toby shut the door behind him and set the key on the nightstand. "Are you going to be okay?"

"Someone bombed the lab with me in it and tried to kill me last night," she said. "And again, today at the hospital."

He sat opposite her on the other bed. "You remember?"

"No. I just thought saying it out loud would help me process it. Or something."

"Right."

"It didn't work. I'm sorry."

"Sorry for what?"

"For not remembering." Tears spilled over her lashes before she could stop them.

He moved to sit beside her and pulled her against his chest and just let her cry. When her sobs quieted to sniffles, he handed her a tissue from the box on the nightstand.

She took it with her bandaged right hand and turned away to mop her face. "Sorry."

"Stop apologizing. None of this is your fault."

A knock on the door jerked him to his feet and she squelched a scream. He squeezed her shoulder. "It's okay. That's probably Amber. Bad guys don't knock. Usually."

She immediately mourned the loss of his arms but quickly focused on the woman now stepping through the open door. "Hi," Amber said.

Robin offered the pretty dark-haired woman a wan smile. "Hi."

"Having a rough day, I hear." Her blue eyes flashed her sympathy.

"You could say that."

Amber nodded to Toby. "I've got this. Go take care of whatever it is you need to do."

"Thanks." With one look back at Robin, he slipped out of the room.

Amber engaged the dead bolt, then took the chair near the window. She placed a gun on the table in front of her, and Robin drew in a deep breath. "I'm going to take a shower if that's all right."

"Can you manage with your hands?" Amber asked.

"Yes. The cuts aren't too bad and Toby's bringing more bandages just in case."

"Okay. I don't think he'll be too long. I'll knock on the door when he gets back with the clothes."

"Thanks."

Toby didn't plan to be more than thirty minutes. Less, if possible. The store was right across the street from the motel. He parked and noted that while he didn't see anyone following him, he wasn't completely convinced he wasn't being watched.

But how? And by whom? With the hair on the back of his neck spiking, he made his way into the store, grabbing a cart and glancing into the mirror that hung at the entrance.

No one behind him looked suspicious. Two teenagers who could use a haircut, a young couple with a toddler and an elderly couple who held hands.

Bypassing the rows of Christmas decorations and aisles of toys, he headed straight for the toiletries section where he pulled up the list Robin had made for him in his notes app.

And then the man next to him caught his attention.

He'd pulled in two spaces down in the parking lot just as Toby had exited his own vehicle. Nothing about him suggested Toby should be alarmed, but just the fact that he was there was enough to make him keep his eyes peeled.

From the corner of his vision, Toby kept the man in his sights while he headed to the women's clothing section and found three long-sleeved T-shirts. He added them to his cart with a subtle glance over his shoulder. No sign of the man. Next, jeans. He found Robin's size and added two pairs.

Another glance around.

The guy was back. This time looking at the shirts on the rack behind him. Toby pulled his cell phone from his pocket and activated the camera as though he were going to take a selfie. He turned his back to the man and lifted the phone to an angle that had his shadow behind him.

Trying to be subtle but needing a good picture, he shifted so it wouldn't look like he was doing exactly what he was doing. He waited until the guy turned slightly, snapped the picture, then held the phone to his ear. "Yeah," he said to the device. "I can do that. Bye." Tucking the phone back into his pocket, he shot another look down the aisle. The person was gone.

One by one, he added items to the cart until he had everything, still keeping an eye out for the guy.

In spite of the fact that Christmas was just around the corner, the store was only moderately busy and within another ten minutes, he was checked out.

And looking for his tail.

Not seeing him but wanting his hands free, Toby transferred everything to the overnight bag he'd purchased and pocketed the receipt. With the bag slung over his left shoulder and his right hovering near the weapon in his shoulder holster, he walked out of the store, tension running through every muscle in his back.

He wanted to know who that man was and if he was connected to Robin. And if he was, Toby was going to deal with him.

FOUR

Robin paced the small motel room while the news played clips of the lab burning in the background. She'd watched it intently, hoping to spark some sort of recognition, but the yawning black hole in her memory never closed. When the reporter continued to say the same thing she'd said five minutes ago, Robin had finally shut the sound off.

Toby hadn't yet returned with her clothes, so she'd wrapped herself in the snuggly robe she'd been surprised to find hanging on the back of the bathroom door.

Amber looked up from the table in the corner. "You took a hard hit to the head. You should probably be resting."

"I can't rest. I need to think, but my thoughts are so jumbled." Robin pressed a hand to her pounding head.

"You have a concussion. I'm sure that's part of it."

"So, after I heal from the concussion, will I remember what happened?"

"I don't think anyone can tell you that. I suppose time will help. What did the doctor say?"

"That time will help." She shot her new friend a rueful smile. Then frowned. "Unfortunately, I don't think I have a lot of time."

Lights flickered behind her eyes. She blinked, then

lowered her lids as she sat on the edge of the bed. No, not lights. Flames. Smoke. Choking her. She gasped and opened her eyes.

Amber stood, brows drawn in concern. "Are you okay?"

Robin raked a hand through her drying hair. "Yes. I think I just... I don't know. Remembered the fire. Maybe."

"Anything else?"

"Choking on the smoke. Feeling like I couldn't breathe."

"I would think that's normal. You were trapped, right?"

"I... Yes. I mean, I think so." She frowned. "Was I?"

"That's what Toby said. He said you broke the window out of one of the bathrooms and escaped that way."

"Then I guess that's true." She pressed her palms against her eyes, then lowered them with a sigh. "So, what do you do when you're not guarding people?"

Amber smiled. "I take care of my family. I have a nine-year-old son and a one-year-old daughter."

"I'm taking you away from your family. I'm so sorry!" Remorse had a bitter taste.

"Hey, it's okay, really," Amber said, her voice low and soothing. "It's been a while since I've gotten to help out and I'm glad to do it."

"Still..."

"No, not 'still.' It's fine, I promise."

Robin sighed. "Well, thank you. I appreciate it."

"Any big Christmas plans?" Amber asked.

Was the change of subject an attempt to get Robin's mind off everything? Possibly. "No big plans." At least she didn't think so. If this Christmas followed true to the pattern of past ones, she would be curled up somewhere on a sofa watching *It's a Wonderful Life*. "I suppose my plan is to stay alive to *see* Christmas."

"An excellent plan."

"What about you? Any favorite Christmas traditions?"

"Mmm," Amber said. "Yes. My family loves Christmas. We usually gather at my parents' house, eat too much, watch football, play some football if the weather cooperates, take a horse ride, play in the snow…" She shrugged. "Stuff like that."

"Sounds idyllic," Robin said softly. Sounded exactly what she'd always dreamed of Christmas being—but not one she'd ever experienced. Longing welled and she cleared her throat. "Toby said you were in law enforcement before. What branch?"

"I used to work for one of the government agencies."

"So, you'd rather not say."

Amber gave her a faint smile. "Not unless it will help you feel better."

"You don't have to tell me." She figured it was probably the CIA or something like that. "Do you miss it?"

The woman shrugged and glanced out the window before turning back. "Sometimes. But I'd miss my family more if I were still working, so I help out some friends who are still active every now and then."

"Like Toby?"

"Like Toby."

Robin pressed a hand against her aching head. "I wonder where he is."

Toby stashed the bag in the back seat and scanned the area one more time. The guy was gone, and Toby started to wonder if he'd been overreacting in the store.

When his phone rang, he yanked it from his pocket and glanced at the screen. "Yeah, Ben, what's up?" He turned his attention to the parking lot, the cars leaving and arriving, the people loading their bags. The guy's car was still in its spot.

"The fire at the lab's been ruled arson."

He walked to the back of the vehicle and noted the license plate. "That didn't take long."

"ATF guys found bomb materials. They've been shifting through everything with the dogs."

"Can't say I'm surprised." In fact, he would have been surprised to hear otherwise.

"So, right now, we're looking for someone who has the motive to blow it up," Ben said. "What was going on in there that someone wanted to get rid of?"

"I've already passed on to you everything I know." Which hadn't been much. Ben already had the background on all of the employees, including as much personal information that Toby had been able to dig up.

"Hold on a second," Ben said. "I've got a text coming through."

While Ben checked his messages, Toby did a three-sixty, still on high alert. There was nothing there to alarm him and yet he couldn't shake the feeling of being watched. He pushed the cart to join the others in the designated area.

"Toby?" Ben was back on the line.

"Yeah?" He headed back to his truck, his nerves itching.

"Alan Roberts and another man were found dead at the scene. They both had bullet holes in them."

"Great. Just great. Who's the other guy?"

"Not sure. They're still trying to ID him. May have to use dental records."

"Alan has a family," Toby said softly. "And a little girl fighting leukemia."

"Oh boy." Ben sighed.

"Yeah." Toby frowned and took another look around the parking lot. It was busy, with a steady stream of people. "Once we know the identity of the other guy, maybe we'll know why they were killed."

"I hope to have that information soon. How's Robin?"

"Hanging in there, but she doesn't remember anything that happened at the lab."

"Nothing?"

"No. Seems like she's lost the last six months of her life at the moment."

"You're kidding."

"I wish."

"Fabulous." Ben paused. "We need her to remember."

"I know, but right now, she's so stressed and shaken, I don't see that happening any time soon. And pushing her isn't going to help. The doctor said to let her heal and feel safe, and the memories should start to return."

"Toby…if someone tried to kill her because of something she saw, we may not have time to let her feel safe."

"I'm working on that part."

"Yeah. Okay. I guess we don't have a choice. Stay low and keep your head down until I get back to you." He paused. "In the meantime, you find her that safe quiet spot to heal. The faster the better."

"Already thought of that."

"I thought you might have. Where will you be?"

"Wrangler's Corner. It's small and close-knit. If any strangers show up, I'll know it."

Ben fell silent. "That might not be a bad idea. Plus, you have law enforcement friends and family there."

"I do." The law enforcement friends were in-laws, but he counted them as family.

"All right. But let me know immediately if she remembers anything. She's not safe if she can't tell us who did this—and why."

"I know, Ben."

"I know you do," his friend said. "This thing's got me rattled. I never saw this coming."

"I didn't either." Toby kept his head on a swivel, goose-bumps pebbling his arms, the air shifting. "When I get back to the hotel, I'm going to send you a picture of a guy. See if you can identify him, will you?"

"Sure."

"Look, I've gotta go. I don't like being out in the open like this. Talk to you later."

"Be safe."

"That's the plan." Toby hung up and placed his hand on the door handle.

A footfall sounded behind him. He started to turn when something hard pressed against the base of his skull.

Toby froze. The man had been watching. Waiting for him to get off the phone, then striking quickly.

"Where is she?" a low voice demanded.

"Who?"

"You know who. Robin Hardy. Where is she?"

"Who wants to know?"

The gun pressed harder. "I'm not playing, man!"

"I'm not either." Toby bent his knees and dropped in one controlled movement. The gun slid away from his head. In a crouched position, he spun and kicked out, connecting with the man's knee.

His attacker yelled but instead of pulling away, he surged forward and struck out, catching Toby on the cheek with a hard fist. Toby's head snapped back and pain vibrated through him, but he kept his feet beneath him.

"What's going on over there?"

The shout startled him and he stumbled back two steps, just in time to avoid the second punch headed for his face. He grabbed the swinging arm and shoved. The man went to his knees, rolled to his feet and bolted toward the back of the parking lot.

Pounding footsteps from the opposite direction grabbed

Toby's attention. A man in a uniform reached him. Another swept past him in pursuit of the fleeing attacker. "Are you okay?"

Toby touched a hand to his cheek. "Yeah, I think so."

"What happened?"

"I got jumped. Let your partner know the guy is armed."

The officer did so while backing away from Toby. "If you're okay, I'm going to go give him backup."

"Go."

"I'll be back to take your statement," he called over his shoulder.

Toby didn't plan to be around for that. He snagged his keys from the asphalt, climbed into his vehicle and headed for the motel. If whoever was after Robin had found him, it was very possible they would soon find Robin. Time to run.

Robin had dozed sitting upright on the bed, her head against the cushioned headboard. When the door opened, she jerked awake, setting off a pounding in her skull. Ignoring it, she swung her feet to the floor and tightened the sash on the shin-length robe.

Amber stood at the door and hit the deadbolt after Toby shut it behind him. "Did you get what you needed?" Amber asked.

"Yes, but we're going to have to take off. Someone attacked me in the parking lot of the store." He set an overnight bag on the bed.

Robin gasped. "Your cheek! Are you okay?"

"I'm fine, but if they found me there, it's possible they could track us here."

"How?" Amber asked.

"I don't know. I checked the truck for tracking devices, but I could have missed it."

"Not you," Amber said. "What about your phone?"

"It's not traceable."

"Everything is," she said. "Even that one."

He frowned. "That would take some pretty high-tech equipment."

"And until we know who you're dealing with, you need to assume they have access to that equipment. You need to ditch it. We'll stop and get you another one on the way."

His frown stayed put, but he nodded.

Robin watched the exchange with a curious detachment. They were obviously good friends.

"Are you a cop, too?" she asked Toby. "I mean, Amber told me she used to work for some government agency, but what about you?"

Toby stilled. "No. I'm not a cop. Although…" He paused. "I have a lot of friends with the FBI."

"Why do I have a feeling it's more than that?" she murmured.

Amber lifted a brow and shot Toby a look Robin couldn't decipher.

Toby sighed. "Although I'm not with an official law enforcement agency, I've—*we've*—both had some training. And we're going to keep you safe, all right?"

She nodded, but something flickered in her midsection. Not fear of Toby, but more of a wariness…an anger? But why? He'd saved her life and was continuing to do so. The feelings didn't fit. Or was her subconscious trying to tell her something?

Toby motioned to the bag that held her clothes and other items she'd requested. "Hurry, we need to get going."

Robin grabbed the bag and slipped into the bathroom. She found the clothes and pulled them on. They weren't a perfect fit but close enough. Next, she downed one of the prescription pills for pain and used the brush to gently force her hair into some semblance of style. She settled for a loose ponytail that didn't pull at her wound.

She was ready. She hoped. Taking a precious peaceful moment, she shut her eyes and drew in a deep breath. Then tried to force herself to remember the explosion.

Heat. Flames. Smoke. Terror.

The knock on the door jarred a gasp from her and she opened her eyes while her heart pounded fast and furious. From the knock or the blips of memory? "I'm coming."

She opened the door to find Toby holding his car keys. "You okay?" he asked.

"Okay might be pushing it, but I'm ready to go."

His eyes darkened with an emotion she couldn't identify. And wasn't sure she wanted to. She was already drawn to this man who'd saved her, but the twinge of…something… that she felt toward him every so often cautioned her to hold herself distant until she could figure it out. She slipped past him and into the room.

Amber stood guard at the window. "I'm going to follow you back to Wrangler's Corner," she said to Toby. "Wait, a car just pulled in the parking lot and slowed when it drove past yours."

"I parked several doors down. They won't know what room we're in."

She held out a hand. "Give me your keys and your phone."

"Why? What are you thinking?"

"Change of plans. I'm going to drive a circuitous route and you guys are going to take my car and phone back to Wrangler's Corner."

"Amber—"

"If someone managed to plant a tracking device on your truck, we need to throw them off. I'll leave it at a bus station, grab a ticket to Nashville, then rent a car and drive to Wrangler's Corner."

Toby nodded. "Tell us when he's gone and we'll go to-gether." He and Amber swapped keys and phones.

Robin stood, bag over her shoulder, ready to act when signaled to do so.

When he tugged on her hand, she followed him to a new blue Tahoe and climbed into the passenger seat. Toby scrambled behind the wheel and within seconds, they were turning right out of the parking lot. Robin could see Amber in her side mirror driving Toby's black Ford F-150. The woman turned left.

Robin watched until she couldn't see Amber any longer and never saw anyone who looked like they were following her—or them.

"You can rest now if you want. It's only about thirty minutes to Wrangler's Corner."

Since her head was protesting in spite of the medication, Robin didn't argue. She closed her eyes and prayed she was making the right decisions, trusting the right people. Because if she was wrong, she was as good as dead.

FIVE

Toby pulled into his sister's driveway with one last glance in his rearview mirror. He'd been on high alert the entire way, and at no time had he seen anything that worried him. While relieved for the moment, he wouldn't drop his guard.

The front of the house shouted that children lived there with small riding toys and a pair of roller skates parked under the wicker table on the front porch. Christmas lights hanging around the perimeter of the door blinked a welcome while the wreath in the center proclaimed Merry Christmas in big red letters.

As a child, Toby had hated Christmas thanks to his dysfunctional family situation. Now, he looked forward to it as much as his nieces did. Which reminded him he still had some Christmas shopping to do.

His sister, Zoe, stepped outside and wrapped her coat tighter around her. The smile that seemed permanently attached to her lips since marrying the town's veterinarian, Aaron Starke, beamed in his direction. Toby climbed out of the Tahoe and went to hug her, then turned and waved for Robin to join them.

Robin opened the door and stepped out next to the SUV, looking unsure and fragile.

"Come meet my sister, Zoe," Toby said. His brother-in-law joined them dressed in his warm winter coat, carrying his medical bag in one hand and his gloves in the other. "And her husband, Aaron." He shook hands with the man. "Sorry to get here so late."

"Not a problem," Aaron said, setting his bag on the wooden floor of the porch and pulling on his gloves. "I was just getting ready to head over to the Wilsons'. They've got a foal who's having some issues, and Bud's worried." He nodded to Robin and grabbed his bag. "It's good to meet you. Y'all make yourselves at home and I look forward to talking when we have more time."

"Thank you."

Aaron kissed his wife and headed for the truck parked near the barn.

Zoe rubbed her hands together. "So, come on in. We've got rooms ready for you."

"Wait a minute," Robin said. "We can't stay here."

"Why?" Toby asked, frowning. "What's the problem?"

"B-because we just can't. What if—" She broke off and bit her lip.

Toby placed a hand on her upper arm. "Excuse us a second, sis."

"Sure," Zoe said. "Just come on in whenever you're ready."

Once his sister was inside, Toby turned to Robin. "What is it? We need you in a safe place. This is about as safe as it gets."

She rubbed a hand across her forehead and he could tell her head was hurting. "But that's just it. It might not be safe. At least not for them. And I'm not willing to put your family in danger."

Toby breathed a sigh of relief. "Is that what's bothering you?"

"Of course. Doesn't it bother you?"

He paused. "If I really thought I'd be bringing trouble to Zoe and her family, there's no way I'd risk it, but no one followed us here. I got rid of my truck and my phone so no one could track us. I really think we'll be all right."

"But—"

The door opened. "Sorry, I couldn't help overhearing," Zoe said.

"Eavesdropping you mean?" Toby asked.

She waved a hand in dismissal. "Whatever. Come inside for just a minute where it's warm so we can discuss this without freezing." Once inside she turned to Robin. "We want to help. I promise we can handle whatever comes our way."

Robin pressed fingers against her temples. "I appreciate it, I really do." To Toby, she said, "But I just… I can't put them in possible danger. If something were to happen, I'd never forgive myself."

"If it helps, we're not going to be here anyway. We're leaving tomorrow shortly after breakfast to go on a little mini vacation. You can use one of the guest cottages," Zoe said. "Toby stayed in one for a while before moving to work at the university. The one right next to it is fully furnished and comfortable. And vacant. Toby can stay in his cottage and you can stay in the other. Both cottages even have some nonperishable food there you can snack on."

"Will that be okay, Robin?" Toby asked.

"I… Yes. That'll be fine. Thank you."

"Great. Let me just get the keys."

Zoe left and Robin clasped her arms to her stomach, the lost look on her face just about doing him in. Toby held still, not allowing himself to go to her. She was a case. He was there to protect her and help her remember.

And he had to keep his heart out of it.

Those last words were ones he'd been preaching to himself from the moment he'd realized she had nothing to do with anything illegal going on at the lab. His head was willing to listen to the sermon; his heart was in compete rebellion.

"What are we going to do?" she asked. "I can't hide here forever."

"Not forever. Just long enough for your memory to come back so you can tell the police what happened at the lab."

"What if it doesn't?" she cried. "What if I can't remember? What if—" A sob slipped from her.

The tears did him in. He slipped his arms around her and she let her head drop to his shoulder just as Zoe stepped back into the room. "Aw, come on, Robin, it's going to be okay. We'll figure it out."

"Before someone else gets hurt?" she mumbled.

"That would be best, yeah." He lifted his gaze and locked on Zoe's very expressive eyes. Toby simply stared at her. She cleared her throat and Robin pulled away.

She swiped under her eyes, then her cheeks and sighed. "I'm sorry."

"Nothing to be sorry for," Toby said. "I think you've earned the right to have a good cry."

A low laugh escaped her, but it lacked humor. "Maybe so. But tears never solved anything."

"You ready to see your temporary home?" Zoe asked.

"Sure." Robin's shoulders straightened and she blew out a breath. "That would be great. I…ah…don't have any money right now, but I can pay you as soon as I—"

"We're not worried about that."

"Unca Toby! You here!" He turned just in time to catch the little two-year-old missile who launched herself into his arms.

"Gracie, you're not supposed to be out of bed," Zoe gently scolded her daughter.

Gracie wrapped her arms around Toby's neck tight enough to choke him. "Unca Toby. Mine."

"Let go, monkey, you're choking me," he said.

She loosened her hold and patted the pocket on the front of his T-shirt, then jammed her hand in. "No candy?"

The befuddled expression on her face almost made him laugh in spite of everything. "No candy tonight. Sorry, kiddo."

Her lip poked out, then she rubbed her eyes and laid her head on his shoulder. "Talk an' walk, pweese."

Zoe bit her lip and held out her hands as though to take the child from Toby. "I'll just put her back in bed and then we'll head over to the cottages and get you settled."

But Gracie was having none of it. "No! Want Unca Toby! No, Mommy!"

With pursed lips and a furrowed brow, Zoe looked at her child in exasperation.

Toby shook his head. "Robin, are you okay if I handle this?"

She blinked, looking tired and dazed and he felt guilty for even asking. "Of course." Then her eyes softened and she smiled. "I'll be fine for a few more minutes."

"I can just show Robin to her place while you take care of my strong-willed child," Zoe offered.

"No," Toby said swiftly. "I'd rather you not. I don't want to leave her alone right now."

His sister hesitated, her gaze bouncing back and forth between the two of them. She finally sighed. "Fine. In the interests of time and to avoid a complete meltdown, it will be easier to let her have her way this time."

"Exactly," Toby said. He winked and turned his attention to Gracie while Zoe linked her arm with Robin's and led her to the kitchen. "Let's get you some water and a bite to eat if you're hungry. He won't be long. He's like a baby whisperer or something."

Toby chuckled and started a silly monologue that would put Gracie to sleep within minutes. But while he paced and talked, his mind churned.

What if Robin couldn't remember what happened at the lab? How would they go about finding the killer? They needed a plan and soon.

Twenty minutes later, he walked into the kitchen to find Robin and Zoe sitting and talking. To say Robin looked tired was an understatement. The strain around her mouth said she was at the end of her rope. The concern on Zoe's features said she was thinking the same thing.

He forced a smile to his lips. "She's out. Robin, are you ready?"

"Yes, please. Zoe very graciously offered to let me lie down, but I'm afraid once I do, I won't be able get up for a while."

"That's no problem." Zoe stood and gathered a few items from her refrigerator and dropped them into a plastic bag. "I've got the keys and some chicken salad and fruit. Let's go."

Toby plucked the keys and the food from his sister's fingers. "I've got this. You make sure the little one doesn't wake up and come looking for you."

Zoe rolled her eyes but nodded. "Fine. If you need anything, you know where to find me."

Toby nodded. "Now," he said to Robin. "We can go get you settled."

Settled would be nice. Because Robin had been *un*settled ever since she'd awakened in the back of Toby's car. And maybe if she was able to sleep, some of the pounding in her head would ease. Toby drove her the short distance to the cabin and unlocked the front door for her. "Here it is. Home sweet home. Let me give you the tour."

"I think I can probably find my way around."

"Humor me. It won't take long."

She gave him a tired smile.

"You're standing in the living area," he said. "Kitchen and laundry to the right. In the refrigerator, you'll find water bottles, soda and probably some chocolates. In the pantry, there are crackers and other nonperishables that will keep you from starving. We'll go to the grocery store in the morning or raid Zoe's fridge."

Robin nodded to the bag in his hand. "I think she already raided it."

"True enough." He set the bag on the counter. "Bedroom and bath to the left. Through the sliding glass doors in the living area is the deck that overlooks the new manmade lake."

"It's lovely. And it's so clean. I didn't think anyone was using this during the winter."

"They're not. Aaron and Zoe have a cleaning crew that comes in after guests leave in the summer and twice a month during the winter to keep the cottages fresh." He smiled. "Because sometimes they get a winter guest or two and want to be prepared."

She set her bag on the sofa. "I really appreciate this, Toby. Please be sure Zoe knows."

"She knows." He walked to the door. "Come here."

"What?" Robin stepped over next to him and he pointed.

"See that cabin right there next to yours?"

"Yes."

"That's where I'll be." He turned back her. "You have your phone, you also have a landline on the wall in the kitchen. Your back door opens up to mine. The cabins are exactly the same, just opposite floor plans. If anything happens, I'll be right here."

"Okay."

"And one more thing." He pointed to the box on the wall next to the door. "This is an intercom system that works between cabins. Zoe and Aaron just put it in last year. Cell phone reception is usually okay, but if the weather gets bad or a cloud gets too low or a bird flies just right, it can turn spotty."

"You're being sarcastic, I think."

He shot her a quirky grin. "Yeah. You never know when you're going to have service and when you're not. Aaron and Zoe have a satellite phone just in case. But at least with the intercoms, there's no problem with us communicating."

"What if the power goes out?"

"There's a generator. It automatically kicks in."

"That's comforting."

"Good. Now, why don't you get some sleep while I head over and check out my digs?"

"All right. Thank you. For everything."

"Of course." He reached for the doorknob and hesitated.

"What?" she asked.

"I just—"

"Just what?"

"Nothing. Your medicine is in the side pocket of your bag if you need it."

"Okay."

Once he was gone, she locked the door and immediately felt the press of loneliness. As a child growing up in foster homes, she was familiar with the feeling. She hadn't liked it then and she didn't like it now. Tears threatened once more, but instead of letting them fall, she closed her eyes and tried to visualize the lab where Toby said she'd worked. She started with test tubes, then beakers, then a table.

The room flashed in her mind. A poster warning of hazardous materials in the area hung on a white cabinet. The choking smell of smoke.

She gasped and opened her eyes while her head began to pound a nauseating beat. She stumbled to the couch and grabbed her bag, shook a pill into her hand and tossed it back dry with only one thing on her mind.

Sleep.

Because she was safe. For now.

Twenty minutes later, as she turned the bedside lamp off and pulled the covers to her chin, she decided she was fooling herself. Because until the man—or men—who'd burned down the lab and tried to kill her was caught, she doubted she'd be safe anywhere for any length of time.

Toby paced the small area of his cottage, his mind racing, heart pounding. The fact that he couldn't figure out how they'd tracked him to the store bothered him. A lot. He was trained to know that. Either he'd missed a tracking device—which was entirely possible since he didn't have anything but his eyes and hands to search with—or it had to have been his phone. But that shouldn't have been possible. At least not for the average or even above average person.

But if they'd tracked him via his "untraceable" phone, that meant the people after Robin were more dangerous than he'd originally thought. Not that he hadn't taken them seriously, but this new information altered things. It would change the way he planned to protect Robin. Because if the guys looking for Robin were as good as they appeared to be, she wasn't as safe as he'd hoped. And that set his nerves more on edge, cranking up his adrenaline.

Using Amber's phone, he'd sent the picture of his store stalker to Ben with a request to figure out who the guy was. It was good to know his instincts were still on target. And while the man had escaped, maybe the picture would connect him back to whoever had blown up the lab and was trying to kill Robin.

He glanced at Robin's cottage and noted the lights appeared to be out except for the one over the kitchen sink. He hoped she was sleeping. She was going to need it.

Toby settled himself on the couch and closed his eyes. Unfortunately, they wouldn't stay that way. The cottage felt too empty. While he was comfortable with that emptiness, he'd never liked being alone. He supposed he should be used to it by now. He lived alone in his little house near the university, but with the constant activity on campus, he never *felt* alone. He simply had to step outside and take a seat on his porch and someone he knew would eventually come along and join him for a cup of coffee and conversation.

Taken from his home and placed in foster care as a teen, he'd always been the outsider, desperately trying to fit in—and never quite making it happen. Until Ben had recruited him to work for the CIA. From a troubled teen with a chip on his shoulder to one of the top operatives in the CIA, Toby had come a long way and he knew it. He just hoped all of the skills he'd acquired along the way would serve him well now in protecting Robin.

His stomach rumbled and with a groan, Toby rolled from the couch to his feet and stepped into the small kitchen. In the refrigerator, he found a bottle of water and some cheese along with a container of chicken salad. From the pantry shelf, he pulled a box of crackers and a bag of chips then sat at the small pub style table and began to inhale the food. He'd been so concerned about Robin, he'd forgotten how hungry he was.

A knock at the kitchen door had him reaching for his weapon. And then he relaxed. *Bad guys don't knock.* He peered through the side window to see Aaron, Zoe's husband, standing on the porch. Toby swung the door open. "Hey, what are you doing out here so late?"

"I just got back from the Wilsons' and saw your light on."

"Everything okay out there?"

"Delivered a pretty little breech foal. Everything's good for now so I thought I'd come see what I could do to help."

"What do you mean?"

"Robin's in trouble, right?"

"You could say that." Toby paused, but he trusted Aaron. Aaron knew Toby's past and continued to treat him like one of his brothers. "Someone tried to kill her and I think she can identify who, but she suffered a head injury in the blast and can't remember anything from the last six months."

Aaron stepped inside and eyed him. "What exactly is Robin to you?"

Shutting the door bought Toby a few seconds of thought for how to answer that. "She's a friend. For now."

"You're risking your life for her," Aaron said with a raised brow. "That's a pretty special friend."

Toby gave a low groan and motioned for Aaron to sit. "It's complicated."

"Okay." Aaron took the nearest kitchen chair.

"You know I was with the CIA," Toby said.

"Yeah, and you quit to teach at the university."

"I did. But the last few months I've been working with the FBI, which is investigating the campus lab. It came to their attention that not everything studied there was legit. Turns out they were right. Anyway, my assignment was to get close to Robin, gain access to the lab and the people who worked there and find out who was involved with what."

"Ouch."

"I quickly figured out that Robin wasn't involved in anything illegal."

"And you found yourself attracted to her."

Toby smiled. "Yes." He shrugged. "But I couldn't do anything about it until I was done with the case. I wasn't going into a relationship built on lies." A pause. "Still won't do that."

"All right. Then what can I do to help? You can't guard her twenty-four-seven all by yourself."

"I'm going to have to find a way. I plan to talk to Clay tomorrow and see what he recommends. I left a voice mail for him, giving him a heads-up we were on the way but that there wasn't any immediate emergency and talking could wait until tomorrow. I guess he's going to take me up on waiting until tomorrow." Clay Starke, Aaron's brother, had been the sheriff of Wrangler's Corner for several years and Toby had come to trust him, too. "I know that during this time of the year, the deputies are stretched thin with everyone wanting time off for Christmas."

"True."

Toby turned and put the remainder of the food back where it belonged. "I brought Robin to Wrangler's Corner because I know there are people I can trust here."

"Exactly." A pause. "How likely is it that trouble is going to show up here?"

Toby raked a hand through his hair. "I'm not sure. When I made the decision to bring her here, I felt like it would be all right for everyone. At least for a short while."

"I hear a *but* there."

"But I've received some intel since then that made me think danger might show up sooner rather than later. Which means we'll have to leave first thing in the morning."

"But where will you go?"

"I don't know. A hotel or something, I guess. As long as we keep moving, it'll be a lot harder to track her down."

Aaron sat for a moment, clearly thinking what that meant. "Or they'll track you down and trap you with no backup, no help."

"Well, that scenario wouldn't be part of the plan."

"Of course not." Aaron rubbed a hand down his cheek, his narrowed blue eyes serious. "You know, when Zoe was in all that trouble, this town and its law enforcement members came together to protect her."

Toby's jaw tightened. He'd found out about his sister's troubles too late to do anything about it. Her dead husband's family had sent someone after her to kill her. Thankfully, they hadn't succeeded. "I'm glad you were here for her."

"I am, too. But my point is, I think this is the best possible place Robin could be. We'll protect her, just like we did Zoe."

"There's no *we*, Aaron. You're heading out in the morning as planned. Let's leave it that way."

"I wouldn't feel right letting you face these people alone."

"*These people* use guns, Aaron." Toby told him about the two dead scientists.

Aaron raised a brow. "Have you forgotten where you are? This is Wrangler's Corner. We're a little more Wild West and less civilized than your big city people. Just about everyone in this town has a gun and knows how to use it. And won't hesitate to protect someone."

"Good point."

"Thank you." Aaron stood. "I'm going to talk to Zoe when she wakes up about her taking Grace and getting out of town for a while. Sophia's heading out on a ski trip with her homeschool group, so we won't have to worry about her. I'll stay here and help you watch over Robin."

"No."

"What?"

"No. You're not a cop. And while I know you're very capable, the fact remains that you're not trained for this kind of thing."

"I know how to shoot."

Toby sighed. "Look, Aaron, I appreciate you want to help, but I can't let you do that. Don't change your plans. Clay is here and has numerous contacts. We'll handle it."

Aaron looked like he might argue so Toby held up a hand. "It's not negotiable, man. I mean, if you want to stay, that's up to you, obviously, but we'll move so we don't make this place a target."

"No, I don't want you to have to move." Another sigh slipped from Aaron. "Fine. We'll keep everything as planned, but I don't like it."

"What exactly *is* the plan?"

"Like I said earlier, Sophia's leaving in the morning with her homeschool group to go on a four-day ski trip and my mom's agreed to watch Grace." Sophia was Zoe's child with her first husband who died before she and Aaron had met. Aaron had adopted Sophia. He stood. "Stay here. Use the house or the cottages, whatever you need. I know Clay and Amber will help you."

"I'm thinking about calling Oliver, too." FBI Special Agent Oliver Manning and Toby had worked together with Ben in the CIA before the other two men had decided they needed a change. They'd tried to convince Toby to follow, but he'd wanted out altogether.

"How's he doing?"

"It's hard for him." Oliver's wife had died and Toby blamed himself for her death—even though no one else did. He stood and walked Aaron to the door. "Lance might not appreciate me involving Amber in all of this." Lance was Amber's husband and a deputy for the town.

"Lance is a big boy," Aaron said. "He can take care of himself and Amber, too." He paused. "Although, I'd say Amber's pretty good at taking care of herself."

"True."

"Just promise me that you and Robin will use the place and do whatever you need to do to help her heal and recover her memories."

"Yeah." Toby nodded. "All right, it's a deal."

"Joshua Crawford is the doctor in town."

"I'd heard he'd taken over for Doc Anderson."

"He did. You might want to let him check out Robin. The guy might be a small-town doctor now, but he's got big-city training."

"I'll run it past her."

Aaron opened the door and stepped out onto the porch. "Oh, and I'll leave you instructions on how to take care of the animals."

"Wait, what—?"

But Aaron was already gone.

Toby shook his head. He'd walked right into that one. But it was for the best. His phone buzzed. "Ben?"

"Hey, I've got something for you to talk to Robin about."

"What's that?"

"The arson team found a piece of paper outside the lab. It looks like there's some kind of formula or partial formula or something. I'm no scientist. I was wondering if you'd show it to Robin and see if she can tell me what it is. I'm sending you a picture of it now."

Toby's borrowed phone pinged. "Got it. I'll ask her first thing in the morning."

"Thanks."

"Hey, what do you think about asking Oliver to help out?"

A pause. "Might not be a bad idea. He works a lot, staying busy and all that."

"Yeah, I know."

"Couldn't hurt to touch base with him and see if he's even available."

"I'll think about it."

"You do that. I'll be in touch."

They hung up and Toby scraped a hand down his cheek, absently noting he needed to shave.

When the text arrived, he took a look and shook his head. The formula made no sense to him, but maybe Robin would be able to tell him what it belonged to.

So…for tonight, he'd keep an eye on Robin. Tomorrow, maybe she'd remember who wanted her dead. While it would be good to have a name, the thought of her remembering still scared him to death because if she remembered that, she'd remember why she'd kicked him out of her life.

SIX

Robin woke slowly, hunger pains pulling her from the dark abyss. The fact that her body was one huge ache might have had something to do with waking her, as well.

For a moment, she simply stayed still, trying to remember. Her head pounded with the effort, and she reached for the bottle of pain medication and the glass of water she'd placed on the end table before crawling beneath the covers.

Downing the pill with a gulp of water, she mentally ran though the food she had and decided on some fruit and…something else.

Moving her head as little as possible, she pulled on the clothes she'd briefly worn last night and headed for the kitchen.

A buzzing from the intercom near the front door turned her steps. She pressed the button. "Yes?"

"Good morning, sleepyhead," Toby said. "It's ten o'clock. I hope that means you slept well."

"Ten o'clock! No wonder I'm starving."

"Meet me outside in ten minutes. Aaron texted and said Zoe fixed a feast."

Her stomach rumbled at the word *feast*. "Okay."

In nine minutes, she stepped out of the cottage and

found Toby sitting in the chair on the porch opposite hers. He stood. "How's your head?"

"Pounding, but at least it's a dull one, not sharp and nauseating."

"Maybe some food will help."

"And coffee."

"Definitely coffee." He paused. "Are you supposed to drink coffee with a concussion?"

"I don't know. Let's find out."

"Sounds good to me, but first, I have something to show you. Ben sent me a picture of a piece of paper found outside the lab. It looks like a formula of some kind." He tapped the screen of his phone, then turned it so she could see.

She frowned. "It's not a formula, it's the structure for a virus."

"What virus?"

"I'm not sure, but it looks like the matrix contains about eight viral RNAs," she murmured. She continued to dissect the structure and finally drew a blank. "It's definitely a virus of some sort, the flu, but I don't know what these add-ons are. Can you print it out somehow so I can study it?"

"There's a printer in Aaron's home office. I'll send it there and you can grab it after breakfast." He tapped the screen. "Done. Now, let's go eat."

Once inside the main house, Robin settled into a comfortable ladder-back chair and inhaled the aroma of eggs, bacon, sausage, hash browns and fried ham steaks. "Wow. Feast is right." Hunger hit her hard and fast. She was ready to dig in but didn't want to seem rude.

Aaron said a quick blessing.

"Where are the kids?" Toby asked as he helped himself to a heaping spoonful of eggs.

"Mom came by and got them about an hour ago. She dropped Sophia at the church to catch the bus with the other kids and then took Grace on home with her. Zoe and I are going to stuff ourselves and take off."

Zoe grinned at her husband and a pang of longing swept through Robin. She wanted a happily-ever-after like these two seemed to have. They'd built a home here, filling it with love and laughter—and good food. She didn't kid herself into thinking they didn't have any problems or life struggles, but at least they had each other to lean on during the hard times.

The kitchen opened into the great room where a large mantel dominated the area. Christmas stockings lined the wood, and a wreath hung in the center. The tree in the corner blinked with multicolored lights and presents surrounded the base of it. Robin decided this was what a home built with love looked like.

"Robin?"

She blinked and focused on the three people staring at her. "Oh, I'm sorry. I got lost in my own thoughts there for a moment. What'd I miss?"

Zoe smiled. "I was just making sure you had everything you needed in the cottage."

"Yes, thank you. It's lovely."

"And you're about my size. I know it may seem weird or awkward, but if you need to raid my closet while we're gone, feel free. Toby said you didn't have much of a wardrobe."

Robin shot him a tight smile. "I don't, so thank you. I hope it won't come to that but will if I need to."

"Great."

For the next several minutes, Robin listened as Aaron and Zoe caught Toby up on all the family members Aaron seemed to be related to. The one that snagged her attention was Clay Starke. "He's the sheriff?" she asked.

Aaron nodded. "I've already asked him to come on out around lunchtime so you can fill him in on anything he needs to be on the lookout for."

"Just someone who wants to kill me," Robin muttered.

Toby squeezed her hand.

Her memory blipped. They were in the lab sitting at one of the long tables. Toby was laughing and she was cold. He slipped his jacket around her shoulders.

The Bunsen burner was on. The flame grew until she was surrounded by fire and she couldn't breathe. She jerked to her feet with a gasp.

Aaron and Zoe froze.

Toby stood. "Robin?"

"I… I'm sorry. I just had a weird memory and then I was surrounded by fire and it seemed so real. I'm really sorry."

He placed a hand on her arm and guided her back into the chair. "It's okay. The doctor said it would take a while, but that your memory might come back in snippets."

"I know, it's just so…strange."

"I really think you should let Joshua check you out," Aaron said.

"Joshua?" she asked.

"The doctor here in town," Toby said. "We'll head over there and introduce ourselves a little later."

Robin cleaned her plate and didn't hesitate to help herself to seconds of the eggs and bacon. When she was finished, she placed her napkin on her empty plate and gave a contented sigh. "Thank you so much."

"Of course." Zoe stood. "I'm going to get this kitchen cleaned up and then we're out of here."

"I'll help," Robin said.

"Nope. You're going to rest that head of yours. I can tell it's still hurting."

"I took some medicine. Hopefully, it'll kick in soon." Robin took her plate to the sink and looked out the window. "Someone's here."

Toby bolted to the window, hand on his weapon. Then he relaxed a fraction. "That's Amber."

Robin flushed. "Of course."

"She came to get her phone back, I'm sure."

"Not to mention her vehicle," Robin said.

"Yeah, that, too. I hope she brought phones for each of us."

Toby opened the door and Amber stepped inside. "Hi, guys, how's it going?" she asked.

"We're safe for now," Toby said. He handed her the phone and the keys to her Tahoe.

She slid them into her jacket pocket, then hung the coat on the rack near the door, then handed him a bag. "Two phones in there. Your truck is safely parked at the bus station. Any food left?"

Aaron walked over to his sister and kissed her head. "Always for you, Mooch."

Amber scowled at him but grabbed a plate and filled it. "I hear Mom and Dad have baby duty for the next few days."

"Yep. And you get to help with the animals," Aaron said.

She grinned. "You think that's a problem? Sam already wants to move in here."

Robin's gaze bounced between the siblings, wishing she could understand that special dynamic they shared. But foster care hadn't been kind to her in that regard. At the age of seventeen, she'd graduated high school early, gotten a full ride to Vanderbilt University and had graduated with honors from there. All by herself. She lifted her chin. She hadn't needed anyone.

Her chin lowered.

But that didn't mean she hadn't *wanted* someone, she silently admitted. A family to call her own. She looked away, her gaze snagging on Toby's. His brow furrowed and his eyes seemed to question if she was all right.

Sharp pain shafted through her head, and she blinked at the vision of the two of them sitting on a porch, rocking and laughing. And then she was curled in a recliner alone and crying herself to sleep.

She shuddered. Was any of it real? Why would envisioning herself with Toby make her want to cry?

Her heart beat a fraction faster, and she vowed to listen to that inner voice that kept trying to send her warnings not to get too involved with the man. While she fought for her life, she didn't need to worry about having to repair a broken heart, too.

Toby couldn't tell what Robin was thinking while he cleaned the second stall of the morning. After Amber had left, he'd retrieved the printed paper with the virus structure on it, then decided he needed something to take his mind off the guilt he was feeling in not telling Robin everything he knew. Even though it was for her own good, the feeling persisted. Because if he was completely honest, he'd admit not telling her everything was a form of self-protection, as well.

She'd been so angry with him when she'd found out he'd been assigned to use her to gain access to the inner workings of the university lab. So very angry. And hurt. Robin was usually slow to anger, but the email detailing his deception had set her temper off faster than a match to gasoline.

And he couldn't blame her.

He hadn't exactly been happy about the whole thing either but had been convinced to go along with it for the greater good. Just like when he'd been active in the agency.

Unfortunately, that didn't help him now. As an ex-CIA operative, he'd reminded Ben that the agency didn't deal with domestic threats, but that hadn't stopped Ben from asking for his help.

"I'm FBI now, Toby," Ben had said, "and I need your help to discover exactly what's going on at the lab. Robin Hardy seems like a good person, but that doesn't mean squat. I've been fooled before. You already have an in since you're an employee of the university. It would take too long to get someone else on the inside."

"Fine. I'll look into her and the lab. Unofficially."

"Of course."

Toby leaned the pitchfork against the wooden stall and glanced at Robin. She'd joined him about an hour ago, tucking the paper into her pocket. "You figure out anything about that formula?" he'd asked.

"Not really. I'll keep studying it when I can. When I try to focus too long, my eyes blur and my head hurts."

She'd resisted his encouragement to rest and he'd let her be. Now, she tilted a water bottle to her lips and drank deeply. When finished, she sighed and drew an arm across her forehead. While it was cold outside with the threat of snow hanging in the air, the barn was much warmer.

"Are you all right?" he asked her.

"Fine."

"How are your hands?"

She still had them bandaged, but they didn't seem to bother her too much. "They're fine, too."

"Would you tell me if they weren't?"

She gave him a tired smile. "Yes."

"Do I sound like a mother hen?"

"A bit, but it's all right."

"Okay, well, if it's too cold or you want to just go inside and relax, you should do that. You have a concussion, remember?"

"I remember. It's kind of hard to forget." She paused, then smirked and rolled her eyes. "In fact, that seems to be the *only* thing I haven't forgotten. Everything else just slides out of my brain like melting ice cream."

"Ooh, that sounds good."

She blinked. "What?"

"Ice cream."

"Are you kidding? It's freezing, and you want ice cream?"

"I do. Chocolate."

"I would have figured you for a rocky road kind of guy."

"Nope. Just plain ol' chocolate. What about you?"

"Mint chocolate chip."

He raised a brow. "You didn't even hesitate on that one."

"And you already knew it, didn't you?"

"Yes."

"I don't have any trouble remembering stuff before I started working at the lab." She rubbed her temples and grimaced.

"All right, that's it."

She dropped her hands. "What's it?"

"You're going to rest before your appointment with Joshua this afternoon. You shouldn't be out here exerting yourself."

She hesitated, then gave a gentle nod.

And that worried him.

Once he had her back in her cabin and settled on the couch with the remote, a cup of water and a bag of chocolate chip cookies he'd found in his sister's house, he left her with orders to rest. Her eyes were already drooping before the door shut behind him.

Standing on her porch, he pinched the bridge of his nose, blew out a breath as he pulled out his phone and dialed Ben's number. He needed an update.

But, of course, he got the man's voice mail. "Call me when you get a chance, Ben."

As Toby crossed the short walkway that would take him to his own place, he saw a glint in the trees beyond the pasture. And again, a wink of the sun reflecting off of something.

Tension spread across his shoulders. Was someone out there?

With a glance back at Robin's cottage, Toby dialed Clay Starke. Thankfully, the man answered on the first ring. "Clay, are you anywhere near Aaron and Zoe's place?"

"About five minutes away, why?"

"I think someone's snooping around and I want to take a look, but I don't want to leave Robin alone. She's inside and supposed to be resting since she's not feeling all that great thanks to her concussion."

"I'm already on the way. Four minutes out and I've got Lance with me. He can stay with Robin while you and I check out the tree line."

"Perfect."

The light flashed again. What *was* that? Binoculars? A rifle? Nothing? No. It was *something*.

He pressed the phone to his ear and moved so he could get a better look without the person realizing that Toby was on to him. If there was a him.

"Two minutes out," Clay said.

"Park on the other side of the barn so you're not visible from the tree line across from the first pasture behind the cottages."

No answer.

"Clay?"

The call had dropped and now he didn't have a signal. Weird. He put his phone back in his pocket and stayed put, watching for more flashes of light.

In the distance, coming up the road that would lead to the driveway, he could see the Wrangler's Corner squad car.

He turned back to the tree line and wondered if whoever was out there had a visual on the car, as well. He thought maybe not. The house and the barn would probably block any view from that vantage point.

Clay finally pulled in front of the barn. He and Lance climbed out and approached. "Thanks for coming," Toby said.

"Of course. What'd you see?"

"Just some flickering. Like the sun glinting off glass or metal. Or something."

"Where's Robin?" Lance asked.

"In her cottage." He pointed to the one Robin was using. "I think it'll be fine if you just want to sit in the cruiser and keep an eye on the place."

"No problem."

Toby nodded to Aaron's truck. "Since I'm down a vehicle, Aaron was kind enough to loan me his for the next few days. Wanna take a ride?"

"Absolutely. But let's take the cruiser."

Clay and Toby climbed into the cruiser and Clay drove slowly, like he had all the time in the world, but was probably just making sure he wasn't missing anything. "Might be nothing," Toby said.

"I know. Doesn't matter. If you saw something, you need to check it out."

Toby shot Clay a tight smile before focusing his gaze

ahead on the area where he'd seen the flashes of lights. "Appreciate it." Clay tapped the wheel while Toby's eyes darted from one side to the next. "I don't see how it could be anything. I know for a fact no one followed us here."

"I don't know, Toby. When people are determined, they'll find a way."

Toby cut his eyes at Clay. "Thanks for making me feel better."

"You know what I mean."

He did. He also knew Clay was right, which was why Toby was being extra careful and going to check out the area.

Within seconds, Clay pulled close to the place Toby spotted the flashes of light and cut the engine. "Over there," Toby said, pointing.

They climbed out of the cruiser and Toby led the way to a small clearing just behind the tree line. "A good place to sit and watch the house," Clay said.

"A very good place," Toby muttered. His gaze swept the ground. Nothing obvious stood out to him. Except a partial boot print and a groove in the dirt near one of the trees. "Take a look at that."

Clay crouched to peer at the ground, then looked up. "Thoughts?"

"Could be anything, I guess."

"That's a heel with a specific design on it. I've got the equipment to make a cast. Let me get it."

While Clay was grabbing the items from the cruiser Toby examined the other thing that had caught his interest. The groove in the dirt.

Clay returned and set his equipment on the ground beside the partial print. "What's got such a tight hold on your attention?"

"This." Toby pointed and looked up at Clay. "I think it's the stock from a rifle."

"I think you're right," Clay said. "That's kind of worrisome."

A loud crack echoed around them and Toby bolted to his feet.

Clay ducked behind the tree. "Someone's shooting!"

"Yeah! But at what?"

"That wasn't aimed at us."

"No," Toby said. "It was aimed at Robin's cottage."

The loud crack and the sound of shattering glass jerked Robin awake. She shot into a sitting position and tried to get her bearings. Her head throbbed and spun, and her thoughts wouldn't line up.

"Robin! Are you okay? Robin!" The pounding and the yelling on the front door finally penetrated her fog and she hurried to look out, staying to the side to avoid any more flying glass. She spotted a man in uniform on the porch.

"Who are you? Where's Toby? What's going on?"

"Stay down! Someone's shooting from the trees!"

She dropped low, keeping her hand on the doorknob.

"I'm Deputy Lance Goode. I'm Amber's husband, and a friend of Toby's. He asked me to come out here and keep an eye on you. Right now, someone's shooting up your windows. Can you let me in?"

She opened the door. Faster than she could blink, he pulled her to her feet and propelled her into the short hallway. Another pop had more glass raining to the floor.

"They found me?"

"Looks like."

She slid down the wall to sit on the floor, grateful for the safe area even as the despair of being found washed over her. Another shot hit the side of the cabin and she flinched. Blinked as a dead man's face floated into her mind. Robin clapped a hand over her mouth and squeezed her eyes shut. Who was he and why did he have a bullet in his chest?

Lance gave her a gentle shake. "Stay with me, okay?"

All she could do was nod.

For the next few minutes, he stayed with her, requesting backup and hovering over her, his weapon drawn. Another loud crash followed by a jarring boom sent her sideways. Lance went to his knees beside her and smoke filled the air.

"Come on!" He grabbed her hand and they bolted for the back door. As they approached, Lance held her back and glanced out the window. "Toby's here."

He opened the door and Robin caught a glimpse of Toby's fear before it eased slightly when he saw her and Lance. Toby snagged her hand and pulled her from the smoking cabin. Lance stumbled out behind her, coughing.

Bullets slammed into the side of the cottage and Toby pulled her to the ground. Another bullet whizzed past her ear and then Toby had her on her feet with Lance yelling, "Get on the other side out of the line of fire!"

They darted around the corner and into the front yard of Toby's cabin. "We don't dare go in there," he said. "They'll just smoke us out again." His eyes swept over both her and Lance. "You two okay?"

"Yes." Robin coughed, her lungs aching. She glanced back at the cabin. "There aren't any flames."

Another gunshot echoed through the air and his jaw tightened. "Clay sent me to check on you two since you weren't answering your radio," Toby said.

"I was on the radio requesting backup," Lance said. "Clay should have heard me."

"Well, he didn't. I had to leave him going after the

shooter alone, and I don't like the sound of that single gunshot. Go check on him, will you?" He rattled off the location.

Lance bolted toward the squad car while Toby pulled her down the small pathway that led behind the cabins.

An engine roared in the background, and Robin shot a quick glance back over her shoulder. "Someone in a Jeep is coming this way."

Toby spun.

"And they have rifles," she cried. "Aimed at us!"

Toby swerved off the path and hit the small backyard of the next cabin in the row just as the first volley of gunfire slammed into the side of the cottage. "Uh-oh. Sent Lance away too fast. Run. Go. Head for the tree line."

She put on an extra burst of speed, ignoring the fact that her head pounded in time with her feet. The Jeep's engine roared. She ducked between the last two cottages and hit the tree line. Toby caught up and pulled her behind a large oak.

"What are we going to do?" she asked, breaths coming in pants.

"Keep going. I've gotten to know these woods like the back of my hand. We can cut through them and come out at the general store." He led the way and she couldn't help but notice he made the path as easy as possible for her.

"Where are Clay and Lance? Shouldn't we let them know we're in the woods?"

He glanced at his phone. "No signal."

"Is that why the radios weren't working?"

"It's possible they did something to jam the radio waves or the signal's just down. But I'm guessing they did something. Should have gotten the satellite phone from the house."

"You didn't know we'd need it. So, does that mean backup's not on the way?"

"Probably."

She shivered as a gust of wind whipped her hair across her face and penetrated the heavy sweater she'd changed into before lying down. In their mad dash out of the house, she hadn't had time to grab her coat, hat or gloves. A fact she deeply regretted. "Where's the Jeep?"

"Behind us somewhere. They probably saw us enter the tree line and are going to come after us on foot. With no way to communicate with Clay, I can't let him know what's going on, but I'm sure he heard the shots. The only thing we can do right now is keep moving."

So she did, stumbling over the tree roots and limbs that littered the wooded floor. Deeper and deeper until she had no idea where she was or which way was out—and her head spun while her stomach lurched. But at least she was warm. A trickle of sweat dripped down her temple. "Toby?"

"Yeah?"

"My head. I'm going to be sick."

He pulled her to a tree. "Sit."

"We need to keep going."

"No. We can stop. I need to take a look around and assess the situation. Just sit here and rest a second."

She nodded. And sat. And placed her head on her knees until the spinning stopped and the nausea eased. When he came back, he placed a hand on her shoulder. "How are your hands?"

She'd forgotten about them. "My head overrules them."

"Can you go a little farther? Mr. Richardson owns the general store just over that hill and up the path. We can use his phone to call for backup."

With Toby's help, she stood. "Are they following us?"

"I'm not sure, but I still don't have a signal."

"How did they find me? I thought you said I was safe?"

"I sure thought you were. I was wrong and I can't tell you how much that scares me."

SEVEN

"If you're scared, then I'm terrified," Robin told him.

He gripped her hand, careful not to squeeze too hard, and she continued to step behind him. "We need to call for help, then find a safe place to sit down and figure out how this happened," he said. How had they been found? He'd been so careful. His mind clicked through the possibilities, even the crazy ones. Like he'd trusted the wrong person. Ben? Amber? No way.

"Actually," she said, "what we probably need is for me to leave so I don't bring any more trouble to your family. This is exactly what I was afraid of. They blew up the cabin, Toby."

"That was unfortunate, but Aaron and Zoe are well insured and they'll be fine." He paused. "And they didn't blow it up. It wasn't a bomb. They were trying to smoke you out so they could shoot you."

"Oh. Well, that's so much better than blowing it up." She grunted and stepped over the next dead limb. Actually, it probably was. Less costly anyway. "How much farther?"

"Just over the next hill and you'll see the path. How's the head?"

"Pounding, but not viciously like earlier and the nausea's eased. I'm assuming that since my breakfast is still where I put it that I'm all right."

She was a trouper. "We're almost there."

He glanced behind them once more and saw no evidence they were being followed. Toby frowned and led the way to the path. "This is it," he said.

"This is what? The path?"

"Yep. According to the Starkes, Mr. Richardson cut this path out for the Updike kids who liked to walk to his store. That was years ago so it's a little overgrown, but we should be all right to walk it."

"Fine. Let's get on it then."

"We are on it."

"A *little* overgrown?"

He held a tree branch out of the way and she ducked under it. Toby continued to clear the path while watching their backs. "Overgrown might be an understatement, but at least it'll be hard to follow us."

"I don't think anyone's back there," she said with a glance over her shoulder. "You think they gave up?"

"I'd like to think so, but I'm not relaxing my guard until we know for sure."

The tree line broke and they found themselves standing six feet from the store's back door. Still holding her hand, Toby led her around the side only to jerk back when he spotted the Jeep parked in the lot. "Well, now I know why they weren't behind us," he muttered.

"How would they know we'd come here?" she whispered. "*We* didn't even know we were coming here!"

"Educated guess. This is about the only place we'd have to run for help on foot."

They'd done their homework. Or they had some mighty sophisticated equipment at their disposal. Satellite? He glanced at the sky as though he'd be able to see it.

"Now what?" Robin asked.

"We wait a few minutes and see what these guys plan on doing. I don't want to enter the store and endanger anyone." He paused, thinking. "Would you be all right on your own for a few minutes?"

"Maybe." She bit her lip. "Why?"

"I want to see if I can get to a phone. A landline. It's the only way anyone's going to know we need help."

"Of course. The landline won't be affected by whatever is blocking the cell signals."

"Exactly." He scanned the area. "But for now, we need a good place for you to hide."

Another gunshot echoed split the air. "Clay and Lance," she said. "They could be in trouble."

"Which is why we need to get you hidden and I need to get in there and find a phone." A Dumpster edged up to the back of the building. "Come on," he said. "You can hide behind here. Don't come out until you hear me knock on the side of the Dumpster."

"Okay," she said. "What if they come back here?"

"Be very quiet." He helped her behind the bin, then stepped back. "Can you squeeze a little farther to your right?"

She did, and he'd never know she was there if he hadn't helped hide her. "Hurry," she whispered.

"Will do."

He slipped around the side of the store to see the Jeep still there. There were two men were seated in the front of the vehicle and they appeared to be in no hurry to leave.

With a frown, Toby stepped back and hurried to the back door of the store. He'd never used it before but figured it would lead him to the office. If it was open.

He turned the knob with a sigh of relief and slipped inside. Shelves stocked with inventory greeted him. Employee bathroom to the left, office to the right, the main store straight ahead. Since the door to the office was open, Toby entered and grabbed the handset from the base. He punched in 911.

"911. What's your emergency?"

"I need you to put me in touch with the Wrangler's Corner sheriff's office. We've got a shooting. And send fire trucks." He gave his sister's address, heard the line click.

"Wrangler's Corner sheriff's office."

"Alice, this is Toby Potter, Zoe Starke's brother. I've got an emergency. I need whoever you've got on duty to get out to the ranch. Someone was shooting at Clay and Lance."

Computer keys clicked in the background. "Someone is on the way," she said. "What about you?"

"I'm at the general store. The men who shot at us are in a black Jeep Wrangler. They were still in the parking lot about a minute and a half ago. Radio and cell signals are out at least in a two-mile radius of the ranch."

"Got it. You should be hearing sirens shortly."

"Thank you."

"I said, where are they?" The shout came from the front of the store. Toby hung up and stepped out of the office. The door leading into the main store stood cracked, and he crept to the side and peered around the doorjamb.

One of the men from the Jeep held a gun on Mr. Richardson who had his back to Toby. In the mirror above the entrance door, Toby had a clear view of the scene. The older man's eyes narrowed, and Toby knew the retired police officer could handle the intruder. "I told you. No one's come in here."

"And I don't believe you. They cut through the woods and this is the only place they could have been headed to."

"And I'm telling you, I haven't seen a man or a woman I don't know. I've only had regulars in here this morning."

The store stood empty for the moment and Toby realized why they'd been outside waiting. They'd been watching for him and Robin as well as picking a time when the store was empty. They didn't want any witnesses. And by the way the man's finger twitched on the trigger, he was only a few seconds away from pulling it.

Toby lifted his weapon and aimed it at the man's head. And hesitated. If he confronted the man with the gun, he could startle him into squeezing the trigger and killing Mr. Richardson. And he didn't see the man's partner. Toby checked the mirror and every square inch he could see. No sign of a second man, but that didn't mean he wasn't hiding somewhere. If Toby pulled trigger, the second armed man might pull his.

He blew out a low breath and tucked his weapon behind him at his lower back while he moved back to the storage room. Hefting a forty-pound bag of dog food over his left shoulder and leaving his right hand free in order to grab his weapon, he returned to the door leading into the retail area. "Hey, Mr. Richardson, I found that bag of dog food. Thanks for holding it for me. Mom would be real upset if she had to run into Nashville to get it." Throughout his speech, he'd waited, listening, praying he could pull this off. "Mr. Richardson?"

Praying he hadn't lost his undercover skills, he walked through the door like he belonged there. The man with the gun had it hidden. All Toby could do was hope he was only after Robin and didn't recognize him. "Oh, hi. Want me to pay for this now or put it on my tab?"

Mr. Richardson cleared his throat. "Ah, we can just put it on your tab. Why don't you…ah…get that on home to your mother?"

"Sure. Will do."

"Where'd you come from?" the stranger growled.

"From the back. Why?"

"Anyone else back there?"

"Nope. Just me. I always park in the back and help myself." On the last word, Toby hefted the forty-pound bag at the man's head and gave a grunt of satisfaction when it connected with a sold thud. When the guy staggered backward, Toby tackled him, his hand wrapping around the wrist that held the gun. The man beneath him bucked and wrenched free, rolled to his knees and turned the weapon on Toby.

The sound of a gunshot filled the small store. Toby, ears ringing, rolled, expecting to feel the bite of the bullet. A chemical smell burned his nose, but when no pain registered, he looked up to see Mr. Richardson holding his Glock on the attacker. "Bad move, son," the older man said to the wounded assailant. "Bad move."

The man glared and pressed a hand over the growing stain on his chest. "You don't know what you've done," he gasped. "Or who you're messing with."

Toby swept the weapon away from him while the store owner gave a harsh laugh. "I know exactly what I've done." He glanced at Toby. "You okay?"

"I'm fine, but this guy has a friend outside in that Jeep."

"The one screeching away out there?"

Toby hurried to the window in time to see the Jeep make a hard left as three law enforcement cruisers spun into the parking lot. "Yeah, that's the one." He opened the door and pointed. "Go after him!"

One cruiser peeled off. The others parked and hurried to the door. Toby turned back to Mr. Richardson. "You got him?"

"Oh yeah. This is one thing you never forget no matter how long you've been retired."

"Right." And help was here. He hurried toward the back of the store. "I'll be right back. I've got to get Robin."

Robin leaned her head against the outer wall and closed her eyes as the echo of the gunshot faded. Indecision warred with fear for Toby and any other innocents inside the store. Should she rush inside to see if she could help? Or would that just cause more trouble? Like allow someone to snatch her. But what if Toby or someone else was hurt? If it was someone else, Toby would help and she could stay put. If it was Toby…

She had to try.

Robin stepped out from behind the Dumpster and slipped into the same door Toby had entered just a few minutes ago only to see him rushing toward her. "Is everything okay?" she asked. "I heard a gunshot, then sirens."

"Everything's under control. The cops are here and we've got one guy in custody. The driver got away, but they'll track him down soon enough."

"What about Clay and Lance?"

"I'm hoping they'll check in soon. If not, we'll start looking for them." He glanced at his phone. "I've got a signal."

"That means the radios should be working."

"Should be. The Jeep probably had the blocking device on it. Now that it's gone, we're good." He led her back to the main store area where a deputy had the offender cuffed and heading out the front door. "Trent!"

The deputy stopped at Toby's call. "Yeah?"

"Hold on a second." Toby turned to Robin. "You recognize him?"

She studied the square face and granite eyes. Pools of black ice stared back. "No. Not that I—" She blinked. "Wait. Yes, I think he does look familiar."

"You better run, lady, they won't stop coming after you."

Robin wanted to shudder but forced herself to lift her chin and glare back. "Who are you and why are you trying to kill us?"

He smirked and shrugged. "I'm just a hired hand, but you've made someone very powerful very mad."

"Who?" Robin demanded.

"I don't know, I just take orders."

She saw him. Watching her. "I've seen you before. But…where?" Sharp pain sliced behind her eyes and she winced, lifting a hand to press it to her head. "In the woods," she said. "I heard you talking in the woods."

His nostrils flared. "I got nothing to say."

"Get him out of here," Toby said.

"Gladly." Trent escorted him out the door toward the waiting ambulance.

Toby placed a hand on her arm. "You remember the woods?"

"Just a vague snippet. Seeing his face triggered it, I think." Robin turned to the two other deputies. "Have you heard from Clay or Lance? We're worried."

"Yes, ma'am, just as we turned in here. I'm Deputy Parker Little and this is Deputy Ronnie Hart. Clay said the radios and phones have been out of commission."

"That's right," Toby said. "I'd hazard a guess that the Jeep your other deputy went after had some sort of jammer on it. A pretty expensive one since it was a large range block."

"That's pretty high tech," Ronnie said. "And expensive."

"Not to mention illegal," Parker said. "Not that these guys care about that."

"No, they don't," Toby said.

"What'd they want?"

"Me," Robin said.

Toby nodded to the door. "Clay and Lance are here."

Robin let her gaze rove over the two deputies. No bullet holes so that was a relief.

"The shooter got away," Lance said, his lips twisting in disgust. "Had a car waiting about mile from where he was shooting. Hopped in and took off."

"Unfortunately, we were on foot until Lance caught up with me," Clay said, "but I got a license number. We'll run it and see what turns up."

"Thank you," Robin said. "I'm so sorry I brought trouble to your town."

Clay gave a small laugh and shook his head. "Can't say we're not used to it."

She frowned.

Toby shot Clay a scowl. "Not funny."

"Nope, but true."

"What do you mean?" Robin asked.

"I'll have to regale you with Wrangler's Corner tales another time. Like when your head's not hurting."

She grimaced. "That obvious, huh?"

"Yeah."

Clay turned to Mr. Richardson. "Looks like you and I have some paperwork to fill out."

The man sighed and nodded. "Let me just close up and I'll meet you down at the station."

"Nice job," Toby told him.

A faint smile tilted his lips. "I can't say I wasn't scared when he was holding that gun on my head, but now that it's all over, I can admit it felt good to be back in the business of stopping the bad guys." His smile slid into a scowl. "Just hate that one of them got away."

"We'll get him." Toby looked at Clay. "Your cruiser's back at the cabin." He handed Clay the keys.

"Thanks."

Toby took Robin's biceps in a gentle grasp. "Are you ready?"

"Yes." More than. Toby was right. Her head pounded a nauseating rhythm and she needed some space and time to think. To plan. To leave? Where would she go? How would she provide for or protect herself? She didn't even know who to watch out for.

"Come on," Clay said, "Lance and I'll take you back to the cottages and you two grab what you'll need for the next few days."

"What?" Robin asked.

"You can't stay there, it's too dangerous. Too remote. You need to be where we can keep an eye on you twenty-four-seven."

"But—"

"He's right," Toby said. "We'll go back to the office with Clay and figure out what we need to do."

She followed him from the store and climbed into Clay's cruiser. At the cabin, she stepped inside to find most of the smoke had cleared out. Quickly, she packed what little she had—ignoring the fact that everything would need to be washed thanks to the lingering smoky odor—and carried the bag outside where Clay stood, back to her door, hand on his weapon.

Toby shut his cabin door behind him. He had a bag over his shoulder, too.

"All right, you two, let's go," Clay said.

When they arrived at the sheriff's office without incident, Robin heaved a relieved sigh and followed Clay up the stairs. Toby brought up the rear, staying mere inches behind her.

Protecting her.

Gratitude welled, and she blinked against the sudden onslaught of tears. Now was not the time to get emotional. With effort, she was able to compose herself before taking a seat in one of the chairs opposite Clay's desk. Toby dropped into the one beside her.

"I'm going to the hospital to check on our prisoner," Clay said. "See if he has anything to say. I'm guessing not, but while I'm busy with him, Joshua can come check you out," he told Robin. "I saw his car at the office."

"Really, I'm fine. I grabbed my pain medication along with my clothes from the cottage, and it's already helping."

"Nevertheless, I think it's best."

"I do, too," Toby said. "Please, Robin? For my peace of mind if nothing else?"

She gave a small humorless laugh. "Fine."

"Good." To Clay, he said, "I'll take her over there. If we go out the back door, we can walk down the row until we get to Joshua's office. I doubt anyone's watching right now anyway. They're going to have to regroup."

"Sounds good." Clay slid his gaze to Robin. "I know we look like a small hick town, but Joshua's a great doctor. Keeps up on all the latest in the medical field and has a full-fledged lab where he does his own testing for a lot of things. He's gotten grants and worked hard to make sure Wrangler's Corner's medical facility is state of the art. For the most part. The only things it doesn't have are the larger pieces of equipment and the ability to provide around-the-clock care."

"You don't have to sell me on the doctor," she said. "I'm sure he's more than competent—and I appreciate your concern."

Clay shot her a sheepish grin. "Right. Sorry. I talk to a lot of visitors and tourists and that's part of my spiel."

He cleared his throat. "I'm just going to go take care of my prisoner."

He ducked out and Toby took her hand. "I think I'm going to call for reinforcements."

"What kind of reinforcements?"

He sighed and stood. "A friend. He and I used to work together."

"At the university?"

"No. Before there. His name's Ben Little, and we've been friends a long time. He's one of about six people that I trust unconditionally. If anyone can help us figure this out, it's him."

"I see. What'd you do before teaching, Toby? I know it was something in law enforcement."

"Yes. Something like that."

"But you don't want to say what?"

He hesitated. Before he could answer, the door opened and a woman rushed in and pulled up short when she saw them. "Oh, I was looking for Clay."

"Hi, Sabrina," Toby said. He nodded to Robin. "Meet Robin Hardy. Robin, this is Sabrina Starke, Clay's wife."

"Nice to meet you, Robin." Sabrina gave them a shaky smile and wrung her hands.

Toby leaned forward. "What's wrong?"

"My grandmother's on her way to the hospital in Nashville. I need to go with her, but I can't leave the B&B because I have a guest who's supposed to check out and he's not back yet," she said, breathless and obviously agitated. "Clay's not answering his phone, Aaron and Zoe are out of town, Julianna and Ross—Clay's parents—" she clarified for Robin "—have the kids. Amber's not answering her phone and everyone else is busy and can't come. I have one more person to call—"

"I'll help," Robin said.

"Thank you, Robin," Clay said, entering the room. "But I'll take care of the B&B."

The woman spun at her husband's voice, then rushed into his arms for a quick hug. "Oh, thank you."

"Go." Clay gave his wife a gentle shove toward the door. She went out as quickly as she'd entered.

"Thought you were headed to the hospital," Toby said.

"I got distracted making arrangements for his around-the-clock guard. Right now, he's in surgery, so no talking to him right now. I'll head over there when he wakes up. I'll probably be there with Sabrina at that point anyway." Clay rubbed a hand over his chin and studied Robin with a look that made her narrow her eyes.

"What are you thinking?" she asked.

"I think I know where you and Toby can hang out for the next few days."

Toby frowned. "The B&B? I really don't think that's a good idea. What about the people staying there?"

"The last person leaves tomorrow. Three more were supposed to come in, but we'll tell them we've had a family emergency and they'll have to make other arrangements."

Robin blinked. "That doesn't sound like it will be very good for business. And have you forgotten that explosions seem to follow me? I don't think you want to risk that."

"We'll risk it," Clay said. "We're not going to let anyone get close enough to blow it up."

"That might be a bit optimistic," Robin said.

"We have insurance if something happens. But we'll do our best to make sure it doesn't. I just feel like this is our best option for you."

She bit her lip. "I'll go along with it if you feel it's best. And I don't mind helping if you think it's safe."

"I do. And trust me, we've weathered worse. What's

important right now is keeping you safe and letting your brain heal so you can remember. Once you do that, then I think all of this will be over pretty quickly."

"Yes, but I don't think we can rely on my brain to cooperate."

Clay nodded. "I understand. So for now, our priority is keeping you safe. The bed-and-breakfast is less than two blocks up the street. You'll be in close proximity to the station. Across the street is the diner and the medical clinic. There are people everywhere. Even at night since the diner stays open until one in the morning and it stays busy right up until closing. There's usually someone there until around two."

Robin bit her lip and Toby thought about it. "It's not a bad idea," he finally said.

"Of course it's not," Clay said. "I thought of it."

Toby rolled his eyes but couldn't help the smile that curved his lips. He looked at Robin. "Is that okay with you?"

"Yes." She rubbed her eyes. "If you guys think that's the best plan for now, I'll go along with it."

"Great," Clay said. "Doctor first though. Joshua's expecting you. Toby, you take her the back way and I'll make sure everything's good at the B&B."

"Did you learn anything about the prisoner?" Toby asked.

"His prints say his name is Brian Holloway. Lots of priors and an outstanding warrant for a murder in New Mexico." Clay lifted a brow. "He blew up a convenience store with the clerk and a customer inside."

"Imagine that," Toby said, eyes narrowing.

"He's not going anywhere but to prison for a very long time," Clay said. "His partner who was driving the Jeep is a fellow out on parole by the name of Ian Olander. Thanks to the general store security footage, we got a good look at him and were able to run him through facial recognition. He's in the wind right now, but he's not going to get very far. If Holloway talks and leads us to Olander, he could probably help himself as far as how much prison time he actually gets, but I'm not counting on that to happen."

Toby nodded. "I have a feeling he was one of the men there that night the lab exploded, but I can't prove it. I heard two men talking in the woods, whispering, really, but I couldn't say if it was his voice or not. It's just a feeling."

Clay walked to the front door and placed a hand on the knob. "Trent and Parker are going to start patrolling the town to make sure Holloway's buddy's not around. I'll be at the B&B sending our last guest on his way, then I'll head to the hospital to be with Sabrina. Let me know if you need me."

"Fine. We'll check in shortly," Toby said. "After Joshua takes a look at her head."

Toby led Robin from the office and out the back door. The wind whipped around him and he pulled his coat tighter, noting she did the same. "It's just a couple of blocks straight through this parking lot."

The employee parking lot ran the length of the buildings. Most of the shops were separated by a narrow alley. The doctor's office was a stand-alone building with an apartment attached to the far end. Garland stretched around the back door and a large lit wreath hung in the middle. "They decorate the back door, too?"

"That's Kaylee for you." Toby rang the buzzer.

The door opened and a young woman in her mid-twenties smiled at them. Joshua's wife, Kaylee. "Hi, Toby," she said even as her gaze slid to Robin. "You must be the friend with the concussion."

"I am."

Toby introduced them, and Kaylee motioned them inside. "Follow me."

Soon, Kaylee and Robin disappeared into the nearest examination room while Toby took up guard outside the door. He pulled his phone from his pocket and dialed Ben's number. It went straight to voice mail, and Toby frowned. When prompted to leave a message, Toby said, "Ben, call me. ASAP, please." He hung up and rubbed his eyes.

Kaylee stepped out of the room.

Toby straightened. "Hey, how's the troublemaker?"

She laughed. "Robin or Duncan?"

"You have to ask?"

"He's two." Kaylee grinned. "Give him a break." Duncan, Kaylee and Joshua's son, was notorious for finding ways to keep his parents exhausted. "And he's fine, thank you."

"How's Robin?"

Her smile faded. "I think she's going to be okay. Joshua will be here in a few minutes. He's just finishing up with another patient."

"Thanks for working her in."

"No problem. You can go on in and talk to her if you want."

"I'll do that." Toby stepped inside to see Robin swipe a tear. He couldn't stand it. He hurried to her and wrapped her in a hug. "It's going to be all right, Robin."

"You don't know that," she murmured. "You can't promise that."

"I know, but I want to believe it. I have to." He lifted her chin and scanned her eyes, then dropped to her lips before connecting with her gaze again.

Her eyes widened. "Toby?"

"Robin, I—"

The door opened and Toby stepped back, his hand going to his weapon. When he spotted Joshua, he relaxed. The doctor's gaze met his with a raised brow. Toby ignored the heat climbing into his cheeks with a shrug. "I'm a little jumpy."

"Understandable."

"Thanks for seeing her."

"Of course."

Joshua turned to Robin. "Clay told me a little about what's going on with you. Amnesia?"

"Yes."

"Well, I'm not a neurologist, but I've done a lot of study on the brain and I worked with several amnesia patients as an intern so I'm not completely in the dark. Ah…no pun intended."

"I'm glad someone's not in the dark," she muttered.

He gave a short laugh. "All right, well, let's take a look." Over the next several minutes, he put her through a battery of tests. Some were the same she'd done with the neurologist at the hospital. The fact that she could almost walk in a straight line encouraged her. At the hospital, she hadn't been able to do it. Maybe she was healing. Joshua seemed to think so.

"How long do you think it'll be before I get my memory back?" she asked.

"Now that I can't say. I don't think anyone can."

"I know. Thank you."

"How are you sleeping?"

She shrugged. "Restless, as you can probably imagine. It's not so much the concussion as the fact that I can't fully relax because I'm afraid someone's going to kill me."

"I can see how that would be a problem. I can prescribe something for that if you like."

"That's okay. I probably wouldn't take it. For the same reason—afraid I won't wake up if there's trouble."

"All right, I'd like to see you back in a couple of days just to give you another checkup and make sure you're continuing to heal. We can do another brain scan if we have to—in Nashville. In the meantime, take the medicine to keep your headaches under control and sleep as much as possible. I know a lot of people think you shouldn't sleep with a concussion, but it will help your brain heal if you do. Even a restless sleep is better than nothing." He glanced at Toby. "You're staying with Aaron and Zoe, right?"

"We were," Toby said. "Now, we're going to move Robin into the bed-and-breakfast while Sabrina's at the hospital with her grandmother. Two deputies and I will be staying on-site to keep watch while authorities work to track down who tried to kill her."

Joshua nodded. "Clay told me a bit about that. You're really having a rough time, aren't you?"

"I am, but hopefully it won't be for much longer," Robin said. She ran a hand through her hair. "Do you have a restroom I could use, please?"

"Of course. Just out the door to the left. Down the hall and it's the first door on your right past the lab."

"Thank you."

She slipped out of the room and Joshua raised a brow at Toby. "You're in deep, aren't you?"

Toby scowled. "What do you mean?"

"I mean you're wearing your heart on your sleeve. Watch out or the same thing that happened to me is going to happen to you."

"What's that?"

"You're going to wind up married."

EIGHT

Robin ran the cold water over her hands and noted the cuts had scabbed over. Fortunately, they'd been superficial and while they'd stung, they were healing fast. She could only wish her memory would heal so quickly. She splashed her face while her mind raced, then patted her skin dry with a paper towel and took a deep breath. She'd had to get out of the examination room. Having a breakdown in front of Toby and the doctor simply wasn't an option.

Okay, recap.

The lab had exploded with her in it, killing two people she worked with—or at least one. She still didn't know who the other guy was. She'd been there, seen something—or someone—and that someone had seen her. And decided that whatever she'd witnessed was worth killing her for.

The more she tried to remember, the more the pounding behind her eyes increased. But she *needed* to remember and there had to be a way to force her brain to do so.

Flames blipped behind her closed eyes. Smoke. Pain. Fear.

Then nothing.

She waited, hoping for something more. When she didn't get it, she focused on the man Trent arrested at the store. She remembered him from the woods. He'd been talking to someone, but who? His partner in the Jeep? Probably. Did she know them from before?

When nothing else came to mind, she groaned and gave up, turned and slipped out of the bathroom to find Toby leaning against the wall opposite the door. "Sorry, I didn't mean to make you wait," she said. "I needed a moment to splash some water on my face and think."

"No problem. Are you okay?"

"I'm… Yeah. I think I'm okay right now."

"Good. You ready to go?"

Her gaze landed on the lab next door to the bathroom. "But I have an idea first."

"What?"

"Do you think Joshua would mind if I looked around his lab for a few minutes? I want to see if it sparks any memories."

"Don't mind at all," Joshua said from behind her. He shut the examination room door. "Help yourself."

Robin took the six steps she needed to enter the open door. It was different from the one she'd worked in before transferring to the university—and yet, the same. She walked over to the microscope, let her gaze settle on the box of slides. While she was aware of Toby and Joshua watching, she was also keenly tuned in to her surroundings. A young lab tech worked at the station near the sink. She glanced up with a smile, then went back to her microscope.

"And I said absolutely not!"

Robin jerked at the stern tone and turned to see a dark-haired mother frowning down at her son who looked to be about six years old. They passed by the lab's open door.

"But, Mom…" the child whined.

"No. Now don't bring it up again." The mother led her

child on down the hall and toward the exit, but the minor disagreement triggered something for Robin.

"They were arguing," she said.

"Who was arguing?" Toby asked.

"I… I'm not sure."

I need that virus now!

"Robin?"

"Um…two men." She rubbed her temples. "They were talking." *How soon is soon?* "There was something about a virus."

Toby frowned. "You think it has anything to do with that paper that was found with the virus structure?"

"I don't know. Maybe. But we weren't studying that kind of virus. That would be done in a Level 4 secure lab. That kind of virus could kill a lot of people if there was an accidental contamination or something. It wouldn't be legal to have it at the university," she said slowly, "but I guess they could have been studying it, working to strengthen it without anyone else knowing about it." She shuddered. "If that's the case, they were putting everyone in the lab—in the city, really—at risk."

"Yeah. That would not be good," Toby said softly. "You used to talk about your work and I know you were really involved in researching cures for various viruses, but you never said anything about suspecting someone was manufacturing a bioweapon."

"That's what it would be, wouldn't it?" She pressed her fingers to her lips. "We've got to stop them, Toby. If that's what it is, I've got to remember."

"You will," he said.

But would she remember in time? The thought left her with a feeling of terror and the desire to run. To keep on running until she escaped whatever it was that scared her so badly. Only she didn't know where to run. And she couldn't. Not if she had the name of a killer locked in her brain.

"Let's head to the bed-and-breakfast and get you settled in a room," Toby said. "I think you've had enough for today."

"I suppose so."

She followed him out of the medical office only to find Lance and another deputy she remembered seeing at the general store a couple of hours earlier. Deputy Trent Haywood.

Lance tipped his head at her. "Hope you're all right?"

"I will be."

"Good." He led the way across the street from the doctor's office to a large dark blue house with white trim. The wraparound porch with the white rockers begged for her attention.

She looked away. Sitting outside wasn't an option right now.

Once inside the foyer with the door shut behind her, she admired the tasteful decor. "It's gorgeous." With the wood floors, pale yellow walls and white trim, peaceful was the word that came to mind.

"Sabrina's got a good thing going here," Toby said. "She's quite the hostess."

"And now she's losing business because of me." Robin sighed.

"Actually," Toby said, "she probably would have canceled the reservations no matter what. Her grandmother raised her and she and Sabrina are super close. She'd be at the hospital whatever the situation."

"Well, that makes me feel a tad better."

He smiled and checked his phone. "Clay texted. You're on the ground floor next to the kitchen if you like the beach."

"Love the beach."

"That's what I told him." Once again, he took the lead and she soon found herself in the doorway of a room that exuded serenity. A pale blue-and-peach-colored comforter decorated with seashells covered the king-size bed. The lower portion of a glass lamp on a white wicker end table was filled with seashells that matched the bedding. Pictures of ocean life hung on the walls and pale peach curtains covered the windows.

"This is lovely," she breathed. "So nice and peaceful." She set her things on the king-size bed and noted the attached bath. "I'm feeling a bit spoiled."

"You deserve it."

"Hmm. That's debatable."

He took her hand. "You *do* deserve it, Robin. That, and so much more."

The husky tenor to his voice tightened her throat. Why was she so drawn to Toby—and yet felt so leery of getting too close all at the same time? He'd been nothing but good to her. Especially the part where he'd saved her life a couple of times.

"Toby, were we more than friends before the explosion?" she asked softly.

His eyes flickered and he sighed. "No."

"Why not? Because I just get the feeling there's something more. Something between us that you're not telling me."

Again, a weird something shifted behind his eyes and she frowned. "The timing was just wrong," he said. "We were both really busy with our work at the university and while we spent a lot of time together, we kept it on a friendship level."

"So, it was a mutual thing?"

"Yes."

She bit her lip. "Okay."

"But I—"

"But what?"

He sighed again, while he seemed to have some sort of internal struggle with himself before shaking his head. "It doesn't matter. Right now, I need to keep my focus on making sure you're safe while we track down who blew up the lab."

Robin let her gaze linger on his a moment longer before she nodded. "All right." But she still wondered what he wasn't saying.

"I'm going to try to get ahold of Ben once more," Toby said, stepping away from her. "Why don't you make yourself comfortable and catch a nap?"

Robin wondered if she'd be able to. "I'll try, but I also want to help in any way I can. Will you keep me updated?"

"Of course."

He nodded and held her gaze a moment longer.

"Was there something else?" she asked. Did she want there to be? Her heart cried yes. Her mind shouted caution.

"No, get some rest, Robin. You're well guarded here. You really need to get some of that healing sleep that Joshua was talking about."

"I know. Thank you."

He left and she took the time to organize her meager belongings before stretching across the bed and closing her eyes.

Unfortunately, that only brought on the memories of the attack at the cottage. She groaned and pressed her palms against her lids. "God, please," she whispered, "let me sleep."

Toby sat in the main living room of the B&B and stared at his phone. The fact that Ben hadn't checked in left a bad feeling gnawing a hole in his gut. He sent a text. Call me, Ben. Things were getting too intense. From day one of meeting Robin, there'd been an attraction between them. At least he'd thought so. On his side anyway.

The fact that Robin questioned if there'd been something more than friendship between them had stunned him. He'd answered honestly. No, there'd been nothing more. The thing he'd left out was that he'd wanted there to *be* more. Only he hadn't allowed that to happen because of his deception. He'd refused to start a relationship with that between them.

But then there'd been the email Robin had gotten, filling her in on exactly what he was doing at the lab.

He closed his eyes against the memory of her hurt—and fury.

And Ben's advice. "Keep your distance, Tobe," the man had said when Toby had confided his growing feelings for Robin. "At least until you can tell her the truth."

Which he'd planned to do. Only someone had beaten him to it. He'd give anything to know who'd betrayed him like that. Only a handful of people had known the details of his mission and he trusted every single one of them. Which sent all of his warning bells jangling and the dangling question: Who was he trusting that he shouldn't?

He glanced in the direction of Robin's room. He still had to tell her before she remembered, because if she remembered on her own and he still hadn't said anything, he was toast. Again. And if she remembered before they figured out who was trying to kill her, she might very well send him away and want nothing else to do with him.

"You okay?"

He looked up to find Clay standing in the doorway. "Yeah."

"Good. Because you don't look okay."

Toby stood and raked a hand through his hair. "I've got something I need to tell Robin, and I'm struggling."

"What? That you're in love with her?"

Toby scoffed. "No."

"Oh. Okay. Then what?"

"Back up. Why would you say that?"

"You'll figure it out."

"Come on, man."

Clay shoved his hands into the front pockets of his uniform pants. "You're desperate to keep her safe."

"Agreed."

"Right now, you're so focused on that, you're denying the feelings that are there right in front of you. And her."

When Toby started to protest, Clay held up a hand. "Man, I've been there. But you're doing the right thing. Put your emotions on hold until all of this is over."

"Yeah." Why deny it? "There's more to it than that, but yeah."

"Clay?" Sabrina called from behind her husband.

Clay turned. "Hey. When did you get here?"

"I have that big order of Gramma's pies to take over to Daisy's tomorrow." She wrung her hands. "I need to be at the hospital and won't have time to make them. Can you let Daisy know? Or no, I'll just stop by on my way back to the hospital."

"Sure, hon. When are you headed back?"

"As soon as I grab some things for her that I should have thought to take the first time."

Clay's brows dipped. "I would have brought those to you."

"No, no. I didn't want to pull you away from what you need to do. She's doing better. She's stable. The kids are with your mom."

"I'll check on them soon. She's got a houseful."

"She insists she loves it."

"She does." Clay kissed her and escorted her to the door.

And Toby's heart wrenched at the exchange. A conversation between two people who had a history. A love. A life together.

That was so…normal. So family. So comfortable.

And something he wanted almost more than anything. Growing up in foster homes and then being recruited right into the CIA after graduation hadn't left him much in the way of family. Which was why he was so determined to stay close to Zoe's family and the Starkes who'd taken him in like he was one of them.

And yet…he still longed for more.

"Toby?" Clay said.

"Yeah?" He drew in a deep breath to get his raging emotions under control. He'd have to do better. Pull on all of his training to keep from being blindsided like that again.

"Lance and Trent are going to stay close by. I've used some deputy friends from Nashville when we've had a shortage of officers around here. I can give them a call and see if they'll come work a few shifts for me. Parker said he'd stick around to help, too, if we needed him."

"That'd be great."

Clay studied him a moment longer before slipping out the front door. Toby could hear him and Lance talking and then the engine of the cruiser purring before it faded away.

Toby checked his phone again. Why hadn't Ben called him back or answered his text message?

The bad feeling in his gut grew to the point that he needed to get someone to check on the man. He punched in Oliver Manning's number. Hopefully, the special agent could pop over to Ben's and see what was going on with him. When Oliver didn't pick up, Toby left a message and tucked his phone in his pocket.

Would Oliver call him back? Or was he on his own now? Time would tell.

About a lot of things.

NINE

Robin blinked at the sun streaming through the window and sat up with a pained grunt. A glance at the clock had her blinking again. 8:40. In the morning? It had to be. She'd slept all night without waking or dreaming or tossing and turning? *Wow.*

No doubt that was thanks to the stronger pain pill she'd swallowed before stretching out on the bed still dressed in her clothes. She squinted. No, wait a minute. She thought she remembered someone shaking her and telling her to wake up. Toby? Probably. She'd told him to go away, but knew he was just checking to make sure she *could* wake up.

Thankful she didn't seem to be getting any worse, she rose and readied herself to face the day. Twenty minutes later, with her stomach rumbling, she went in search of coffee and food. Coffee being the priority.

Toby sat at the kitchen table reading the paper. He looked up. "Morning. Sleep okay?"

"I did."

He glanced at his phone and frowned.

"What's wrong?" Robin asked.

"Nothing. Just expecting a call from a friend. Two

friends, actually. I'm just a little surprised I haven't heard from them."

Surprised. Perturbed. Worried…

The front door swung open and Toby bolted to his feet. Only to slump back into his chair when Sabrina hurried into the kitchen.

"Sorry, sorry. I'm just here for a few minutes. I have to make those pies after all. Daisy called and said she's already presold three of them." She opened the drawer near the stove and pulled out an apron. Then she buzzed to the pantry and started pulling ingredients off the shelf.

"Sabrina?" Robin said.

"Yes?" The woman spoke over her shoulder, her movements jerky and hurried.

"Stop."

Sabrina froze and turned, hands held midair. "What?"

Robin walked to her and pulled the apron from where she'd tossed it into the crook of her arm. "I can do this if you have recipes. And I—or one of my many efficient bodyguards—can deliver them to Daisy's restaurant."

"What?"

"Are the recipes written down somewhere?"

"Ah, yes," Sabrina stammered, "but you can't… I mean, you're hurt. You should be resting and—"

Robin tied the apron around her waist. "My head is better. Not perfect, I'll admit, but it's better. And I have nothing to do all day except think about all the things I can't remember and then beat myself up about it. So, if you want to spare me that, then let me do something productive."

Sabrina's shoulders wilted. "I'd love to spare you. Thank you," she whispered.

"Of course."

"Okay," Sabrina said, "this is what I need." For the next fifteen minutes, she went into teaching mode with

Robin nodding and promising she could handle it. "But if you get tired or your head starts hurting worse, please don't worry about it."

"I won't. I'll just put Toby to work."

Toby snorted, then coughed to cover it up. Sabrina smiled. Then hugged Robin. "I don't know how to thank you."

"First tell me where Daisy's is so I know where I'm going."

Toby laughed. "I can take care of that part."

"Good." Robin turned back to Sabrina. "Go be with your grandmother and don't worry about this. We've got it covered."

"Okay. Thank you. I just have to get a few more things that she's asked for and then I'll be gone."

True to her word, five minutes later Sabrina swept out of the door—after one more hug for Robin—and Robin turned back to the multitude of pans and pie ingredients. And recipes. "Wow."

Toby stepped up behind her. "Ah, Robin?"

"Yes?" She turned and look up into his eyes. Eyes that held a tender wariness.

"I don't remember you knowing how to cook."

Robin sucked in a shaky breath. "That's because I don't know how, but…"

"But?" he asked.

"But you do."

He blinked, then his eyes narrowed. "How do you know that?"

"I don't know for sure. I just had a mental image of you cooking. Something. A steak and potatoes? Mixing a salad?"

"Yeah." Excitement tinged his voice.

"I was sitting at the kitchen table and…"

"And?"

"Nothing. That's it. But it made me hope that maybe we could help Sabrina together."

He took her hands and her heart thudded. The way he looked at her…like he wanted to hold her close and push her away at the same time.

"Why are you so conflicted?" she asked.

"I'm… I need to…say…" He broke off with a groan.

"Toby?"

He shook his head. "I'm sorry. I know I'm sending you mixed signals and that's because it's all I've got, but let's not think about that for now. All of that doesn't matter at the moment. What *does* matter is getting these pies made and delivered, right?"

Robin bit her lip. He wasn't going to tell her what had him so tormented. Maybe with time he'd feel comfortable confiding in her. But for now, she'd take her mind off the fact that a killer was out there and knew where she was.

And learn how to bake pies.

Toby helped Robin get the last pie in the oven and glanced at the ones they'd already finished and packed into the box sitting on the table. He'd have Lance or Trent carry them across the street to the diner as soon as the three cooking came out.

He breathed deep. "It smells amazing in here," he said. "Strawberry, cherry, blueberry, apple and peach. I can't tell which one I prefer."

"It only smells so good because of you."

He smiled and swiped a finger down her nose.

She wrinkled it. "What is it?"

He showed her his finger. "Flour."

"Because you threw it at me."

"Only because you practically dumped the whole bag on my head."

"That was an accident," she huffed. "You bumped me when I was getting ready to pour it into the mixer."

"I was looking for another bowl." Truly, he'd been distracted by all the fun he was having doing something as simple as making pies with Robin. He'd been scavenging in the lower cabinet when his shoulder had knocked into her leg, sending her off balance. And the flour onto his head.

He shook his hair and a cloud of white flew from the short strands. "I'll never get all that out."

She giggled and he stilled. It was the third time he'd heard her do that during the last two hours and it sent his heart soaring each time the sound bubbled out of her.

Tell her everything!

Robin's giggled settled into a smile. "A good shampoo will do wonders." She went to the sink and grabbed the scrub brush. She paused, looking out the window. He simply watched her, wishing he knew what to do to help her remember.

Tell her the truth.

"Robin?"

"Yes?" She didn't turn to him but frowned, her attention caught on something outside.

"What is it?" he asked.

"There are two guys coming up the front steps. Lance and Trent stopped them and then let them keep coming."

Lightning quick, Toby went to the front door just as the doorbell rang.

"If they were going to kill me, I don't think they'd ring the bell, do you?"

"No. They're not here to kill you." Just interrogate her and try to force her to remember—and possibly clue her

"FAST FIVE" READER SURVEY

Your participation entitles you to:
* ✳ 4 Thank-You Gifts Worth Over $20!

Complete the survey in minutes.

Get 2 FREE Books

Your Thank-You Gifts include **2 FREE BOOKS** and **2 MYSTERY GIFTS**. There's no obligation to purchase anything!

See inside for details.

Dear Reader,

Since you are a lover of our books, your opinions are important to us... and so is your time.

That's why we made sure your **"FAST FIVE" READER SURVEY** can be completed in just a few minutes. Your answers to the five questions will help us remain at the forefront of women's fiction.

And, as a thank-you for participating, we'd like to send you **4 FREE THANK-YOU GIFTS!**

Enjoy your gifts with our appreciation,

Pam Powers

To get your
4 FREE THANK-YOU GIFTS:

✱ Quickly complete the "Fast Five" Reader Survey
and return the insert.

"FAST FIVE" READER SURVEY

1 Do you sometimes read a book a second or third time? ○ Yes ○ No

2 Do you often choose reading over other forms of entertainment such as television? ○ Yes ○ No

3 When you were a child, did someone regularly read aloud to you? ○ Yes ○ No

4 Do you sometimes take a book with you when you travel outside the home? ○ Yes ○ No

5 In addition to books, do you regularly read newspapers and magazines? ○ Yes ○ No

YES! I have completed the above Reader Survey. Please send me my 4 FREE GIFTS (gifts worth over $20 retail). I understand that I am under no obligation to buy anything, as explained on the back of this card.

❏ I prefer the regular-print edition
153/353 IDL GM3W

❏ I prefer the larger-print edition
107/307 IDL GM3W

FIRST NAME	LAST NAME

ADDRESS

APT.#	CITY

STATE/PROV.	ZIP/POSTAL CODE

READER SERVICE—Here's how it works:

BUSINESS REPLY MAIL

FIRST-CLASS MAIL   PERMIT NO. 717   BUFFALO, NY

POSTAGE WILL BE PAID BY ADDRESSEE

READER SERVICE
PO BOX 1341
BUFFALO NY 14240-8571

NO POSTAGE
NECESSARY
IF MAILED
IN THE
UNITED STATES

in on what he was really doing. Not that he didn't want her to know. He did. Just on his timetable, not theirs. If she pushed him away now, he wouldn't be able to protect her. And Ben knew that. But apparently, his friend couldn't hold off his fellow feds any longer. "Stay back unless I ask you to come out, okay?"

She frowned. "I'll talk to them, but it's not like I have anything to tell them."

"I want to avoid that for now," Toby said. "The more stress you have on you, the more it may delay you remembering." He cupped her chin. "And I want to make sure they're legit before letting on that you're even here. Will you trust me to handle this?"

She blinked up at him. "Okay. For now. I'll just clean up the kitchen then."

"Thank you."

Robin disappeared back into the kitchen and Toby opened the door. "Can I help you?"

The one on the left, dressed in business casual slacks and a long-sleeved dark blue sweater, held up his credentials. "I'm Special Agent Donny McBride. This is Special Agent Emmett Young. We're here to speak to Ms. Robin Hardy."

"What about?"

"You're Toby Potter, right?"

"I am."

"We're aware that you were working with Ben Little on the suspicious activities at the university lab. We're not working that case and need to question her about the night the lab blew up. We know the explosion was deliberate and we need her help to figure out who's responsible."

Toby frowned, stepped outside and shut the door behind him. "What do you mean, you're working it now? Special

Agent Ben Little is working this case, and he didn't tell me about this. Where do you guys fit in?"

The agents exchanged a look, and that bad feeling Toby had earlier returned full force. "What happened to Ben?" he asked softly.

"He's dead," Special Agent Young said. "I'm sorry."

If the man had sucker punched him, Toby wouldn't have been more stunned. He registered the words but couldn't seem to process them.

"Sir?" the man said.

Toby finally gasped. Took a breath. Then another. "What happened?"

"Looks like a freak accident," Special Agent McBride said. "Ben was working under his car and the jack failed. It crashed down on him, crushing him and kill him instantly."

Pulling on his years of experience, Toby shut off his emotions. "I see."

"We were assigned Ben's cases, and this one's our priority," Special Agent Young said. "We found your number in a file but can't figure out exactly where you fit in with this or who you are—except that Ben trusted you and asked for your help."

"Which office are you out of?"

"Nashville."

The same office as Ben—and his friend Oliver Manning. Toby pulled his phone from his pocket. "Hold on just a second." He dialed Oliver's personal number.

"Toby? What's up?" Oliver's bass voice came through the line.

"How are you doing?"

"Hanging in there. I miss her every day."

Toby closed his eyes briefly. Oliver's wife had been killed a little over a year ago. Yet another piece of Toby's past that would always be with him no matter how hard he tried to put it behind him. "I know, man. Sorry I've been out of touch."

Oliver sighed. "Don't worry about it. We've both got to move on." He paused. "I'm sorry I didn't call you back. I got your message, but I was in a meeting and couldn't take the call."

"It's okay."

Oliver let out a harsh laugh. "But you didn't call to listen to me whine. What's up?"

"You're not whining. I do have a question for you though."

"Sure."

"Is Ben dead?"

Silence. Then, "Who told you?"

So, it was true. Renewed grief shafted him, and he grappled to get it under control. "Two agents," he said. "Young and McBride from your branch. Creds are legit, but you and I know how much that means. You know them?"

"I do."

"Describe them for me."

Oliver did so right down to the mole on Young's left cheek. "Thanks," Toby said.

"What's going on?" Oliver asked.

"I'll explain later." He hesitated. "Why didn't you tell me about Ben?"

"I figured you'd already know."

"Right. Talk to you soon."

They hung up, and Toby considered the two agents waiting patiently for him to acknowledge them again. "No offense."

"None taken," Young said.

"How did you know we were here?" Toby asked.

"That file of Ben's. There was a reference to Wrangler's

Corner in it. A waitress in the diner across the street told us she'd seen you two here."

Of course, she had. In a small town, if you wanted information, you simply visited the local diner or café and asked.

"Now, will you tell us what you know about this case and what connection you had to Ben?" Special Agent Young asked.

Toby crossed his arms. How much should he tell them? Did it matter at this point? "I was working with Ben," Toby said. "He and I worked together back when we were both CIA."

"CIA?"

"Ben was with the agency for about twelve years before he decided he'd had enough. He resigned and went over to the FBI. But when Ben quit, so did I."

"Why?"

Toby narrowed his eyes, and tension tightened his shoulders. "Personal reasons." Reasons he didn't deem necessary to reveal to the men. "Ben was my handler and one of my best friends. And while I had only been there for five years, I was tired of it all, too. The lure of teaching at the university and living a normal life was too intriguing. So, I decided that I'd try it and see if I could do it. And I could." At least until Ben had tracked him down.

"And you were working with Ben on this case?"

"He asked." Actually, he'd begged. And now he was dead from an accident? Somehow Toby didn't think so. "I was already working at the university when Ben was alerted to a possible threat coming out of the research lab. He asked me to use my skills to ferret out any information I could. Since Robin was the initial suspect, I…buddied up to her." A fact that had blown up in his face along with the lab. If he could do it all over again…

"And what did you find?" McBride asked.

"It was soon apparent that Robin knew nothing about anything illegal going on in the lab, but I stayed with her on the off chance that she might have inadvertently heard or learned something and just didn't realize it."

McBride leaned forward. "And?"

"Nothing. At least not until the lab explosion. She must have heard or seen something that night because someone is trying awfully hard to kill her."

Special Agent Young nodded. "That was what we understood from reading the file. Now, we need to talk to Ms. Hardy."

"She's resting right now. Look, Ben trusted me to help him get to the bottom of this. Stressing her out trying to remember isn't going to help. She's under a doctor's care, those are his orders. Can you just give us a little more time? Time for her to heal and time for me to help her remember?"

Special Agent Young pursed his lips and shot a perturbed look at his partner.

Toby didn't care. His job for now was to protect Robin—and be the one who was there when she remembered. Even though when she remembered the explosion, she'd probably remember why she'd never wanted anything to do with him again. And while last time, he'd been upset and furious with whoever had betrayed him, this time, Robin's banishing him from her life would very likely break his heart.

Robin had been watching out the window for the past ten minutes. Toby's expressions hadn't been encouraging. He'd gone from guarded to pleading to determined. She'd give anything to hear what they were talking about but couldn't figure out how to eavesdrop.

Then was ashamed she was even tempted to try.

Then again, this was her life on the line and attempted eavesdropping was probably the least of her problems.

Finally, the two men turned and left the porch with Lance, Trent and Toby watching them walk away. She opened the door and Toby turned. "Everything all right?" she asked.

"For now," he said and stepped inside. "Lance said he'd deliver the pies over to Daisy."

"They're all ready."

Once Lance had retrieved the pies and left, Toby pulled Robin into the den and she dropped onto the sofa. "What did they want?" she asked.

"To talk to you, of course."

"Of course. So, why didn't you let them in?"

He raked a hand through his hair. "I told them that stressing you and pressing you to remember wasn't going to help anything and they needed to leave you alone."

She raised a brow. "And they listened?"

"For now."

"Who did you call?"

"A friend I used to work with. I knew he could verify their identities. He did."

"Who's the friend?"

"His name's Oliver Manning. We used to work together."

"One of the friends you were waiting to hear from earlier?"

"Yes."

"What does Oliver do?"

"He's in law enforcement. He's with the FBI."

Her jaw dropped. "And you used to work together? With the FBI?"

"No. Not the FBI." He trailed off and his fingers curled into fists on his thighs.

"Toby?"

"They killed Ben," he said.

A gasp slipped from her. "What?"

"My friend, Ben. He was the one who helped us get away from the people who were trying to kill you the night of the explosion."

Robin palmed her eyes. "Okay. Stop."

"What?"

"Stop and start over. Start at the beginning."

He hesitated, the grief in his eyes so raw, she leaned forward and wrapped her arms around his waist and let her cheek rest over his heart. "Oh, Toby. I'm so sorry."

"Yeah. Me, too." He cleared his throat and leaned back. She missed his closeness, his comfort. When he held her, she felt safe and wanted that feeling to go on. Her mind flashed, a memory clicked. She stilled and let it wash over her. She and Toby standing on a porch under the light. Toby leaning in. His lips on hers for a few brief sweet moments, then he was pulling back, regret in his eyes. *I'm sorry, I shouldn't have done that.*

She tumbled from the past back into the present. "You kissed me," she whispered.

He stilled. "What are you talking about?"

"On my porch one night. You kissed me. Then apologized." His eyes slid from hers. "Toby?"

"I did."

"Why apologize?"

"Because I felt like I'd overstepped a line. We were co-workers and friends and I was afraid I'd messed that up by kissing you."

"What did I say?"

"That it was all right."

"I see." She cupped his cheeks and pulled his face to hers. His eyes went wide when she pressed her lips to his. Then he gathered her close once more and settled in to the kiss. She took comfort from it—and it confirmed at least one thing for her. She wanted to be more than friends with Toby Potter.

When she pulled back, he let her go and leaned his forehead against hers. "Oh, Robin, this isn't a good idea."

"So, you're going to apologize again?"

His lips quirked. "I don't have anything to apologize for. You kissed me."

She laughed. "I did. And I enjoyed it." She let the smile slide from her lips. "I like you, Toby. I trust you. And yet…"

"Yet what?"

"I feel like you're not telling me everything."

He sighed. "I'm not."

"Why?"

"Because I'm afraid that…"

"What? Tell me, please."

"I will. Soon. But Ben's death has really thrown me."

She nodded. "Okay. Then talk about that."

"I don't think Ben's death is an accident. It's just too coincidental."

"If it's not an accident, then you're talking murder."

"Yes."

"But why?"

"Because whoever's after you knows he was helping us."

"And who would know that?"

He rubbed his chin. "Someone he works with. Someone he trusted."

Robin caught her breath. "The two agents who were just here?"

"Maybe. They inherited Ben's cases, but that doesn't mean they didn't know what was going on before he died."

"What are you going to do?"

"Watch our backs and do a little digging into the two agents. Oliver said they were legit, but that doesn't mean they're not dirty."

"How are you going to find that out?"

"By enlisting the help of people we know we can trust."

"Who?"

"Clay, Trent, Lance and the other deputies. I know for sure they didn't have anything to do with the events in Nashville. I trust my friend Oliver Manning and a couple of other agents I worked with."

"You were with the FBI?"

He hesitated. "No, not officially. I used to work for the government in a capacity that allowed me access to certain information that the FBI found helpful."

She frowned. "You're being deliberately vague."

"I know."

"So, are you still working for them?" A thought hit her. "Wait a minute. Were you working for them when the lab exploded?"

"Yes."

"In what capacity?"

He stood and strode to the mantel. "Ben thought there might be something going on at the lab. He asked me to look into it."

"Did you find anything?"

"No. Nothing."

"But something was obviously going on. How did you miss it?"

He shrugged. "I wasn't there long enough to really do the kind of digging I needed to do."

"I see." But she wasn't sure she did, and that worried her. Right now, she trusted Toby with her life.

Was she making a mistake that would cost her more than she wanted to pay?

TEN

Toby had chosen his words carefully. He'd told her the truth, just not all of it. Like the fact that he'd followed orders to win her trust and investigate her. And to use her to get information about the people who worked at the lab. No, he couldn't tell her that, yet. Not if he wanted to protect her.

He could tell her he'd been with the CIA, but was afraid that would trigger her memory of the email. The email he was still in the dark about as to who the sender was. He'd tried to find out, but all of his searching had led to a dead end. Which meant the person was highly skilled with technology—or knew someone who was.

The fact that Robin had remembered the kiss and his apology stirred his relief—and anxiety. She was going to remember soon and he needed to find out who was trying to kill her before that happened. And not only that, he now needed to know if Ben's accident was really an accident.

"I need to make a phone call," he said. "I'm going to slip back out on the porch and call Oliver. Are you going to be okay?"

"I'm fine. It's you I'm worried about now."

Her words seared his heart. "Thanks. I'll grieve, but I'll be all right in time." Toby dialed Oliver's number once more and took a seat out on the glider. Lance, seated in his cruiser at the curb, caught his eye and nodded. Toby did the same.

"Twice in one day," his friend said by way of greeting. "To what do I owe this honor?"

"I need some help and information, and I think you're the only one I trust to provide it."

"Well, that's got my attention. This have anything to do with those two agents you called me about?"

"Probably. But first, is there any way Ben's accident wasn't an accident?"

Silence. Then Oliver released a slow breath. "You think someone killed him?"

"I don't know what to think," Toby said. "I just know Ben was helping Robin and me run from a killer and now he's dead. What does that sound like to you?"

"Suspicious when you put it like that. He told me about the explosion at the lab. Even asked me to look into it with him, use my connections and see if I could turn up anything."

"No kidding."

"Nope. He knew we were friends and figured I'd want to help."

"Yeah. Well, now these two agents have shown up and are pressing to get Robin to remember…" Toby shook his head even though Oliver couldn't see him. "Pushing her isn't going to work, and I'm not sure how to convince them of that."

Another pause. "I'm going to head your way," Oliver said. "With the two of us working on this, we should be able to dig up answers—and maybe I can help keep the other vultures at bay."

"You sure?"

"Positive. Although, you and I both know that these guys are just doing their job."

"I know. And I don't want to stop them from doing it. Completely. Let them investigate the bombing all they want. I just need them to leave Robin alone for now."

"I can help with that. If someone killed Ben because of his involvement with you, then you're going to need backup you can trust. Young and McBride are good agents, but as you've discovered, they're not exactly patient. They're going to do whatever it takes to get this wrapped up—including using measures that might not be palatable, if you know what I mean."

Toby did. They wanted to put Robin in a room and question her ceaselessly, to traumatize her poor brain until she either remembered or had a mental breakdown. He'd seen it done before and it wasn't fun. And there was no way he was going to allow that to happen to Robin.

Robin told herself she needed to keep her distance from Toby. A man she trusted but couldn't remember—and yet had kissed at some point in her murky past. So, when he asked if she wanted to walk across the street to grab a bite to eat, her mind said no, even while her lips said, "That sounds great."

With Lance and Trent on bodyguard duty, she'd be glad to get out of the house and do something normal. Forget her troubles. Or, if not forget, at least put them aside for a short hour.

Once settled in a booth in the back near the restrooms, Robin took note of Lance and Trent seated just inside the door. Clay stepped inside, caught Toby's eye and headed for their table.

"All right if I join you two?"

"Of course," Toby said. "Thought you'd be at the hospital. What's up?"

"Sabrina's grandmother is doing much better, so Sabrina was fine with me coming back here. I saw you all walk in the diner and wanted to let you know that I just heard from Nashville. The guy we had in custody, Holloway, died."

Robin gasped.

Toby stared. "What? How?"

"From complications with the bullet wound. Apparently, he developed a blood clot that went to his heart and killed him."

Toby shook his head. "Great."

"Yep. So…we'll get nothing from him."

"And the other guy in the Jeep escaped," Toby said.

"Yes. Same type of rap sheet as his partner. There's a BOLO out on him."

The waitress interrupted, took their order and hustled off with the promise to be right back with drinks.

Toby nodded at Robin. "She's been studying the paper found at the scene of the explosion," he told Clay, "but so far hasn't been able to come up with what it could be related to."

"It's definitely a virus," Robin said, pulling the paper from her pocket. She'd copied it from the picture on Toby's phone. "But I think there's part of the structure missing."

"Like what?"

She shrugged. "I don't have any idea. I can think of several ways to complete it, but none of them have anything to do with what we were all working on."

"Which was what?"

"Cures for cancer. Vaccinations against viruses and super viruses. That sort of thing." Her eyes widened. "Wait a minute, this would create a virus, not prevent one."

"So, create it," Toby said softly.

"What?"

"Create it. That might be exactly what they were arguing about in the lab," Toby said. "You said they were talking about a virus and having it ready. We've already speculated they could have been working on something in secret, creating a virus that could be used as a bioweapon. Can you do that with what you have there?"

Robin shuddered. "How awful." She glanced at the structure again. "But yes, they could have."

"If there was a buyer for it, that could explain what you overheard about having it soon," Toby said.

"Then whoever torched the lab and tried to kill me might have the ability to make the virus and be planning to sell it," she said.

The bidding has already started. I need that virus now!

It's not ready. I told you. I'm still working out some issues, but I should have it soon.

She sucked in a breath and Toby's eyes narrowed on her. "What is it?" he asked.

The waitress returned with the drinks. Robin stared at her hands, thinking. "One of them said the bidding had already started and needed the virus," she said, "but Alan said it wasn't ready." She pulled the structure up one more time. "I need a pen and paper. I don't want to write on this one."

Clay handed her a pen and Toby slid her a clean napkin. She drew the structure as it was on the paper then added more information. She flipped the napkin and continued working, adding various other structures that might work or might not. For the next thirty minutes, she filled up napkin after napkin with her scribbles.

Finally, she dropped the pen and sat back staring at the last napkin, appalled at what she thought she'd just put together. "I don't know, but I think I just created a virus that could do a lot of damage if it fell into the wrong hands. And if I did it that easily, there's no way that Alan couldn't have done it."

She snatched up the napkin and ripped it to shreds, then shoved the pieces into her coat pocket. She'd burn them later. With a groan, she palmed her eyes and let the memories come. "They were arguing. Alan was working on the virus. The other man said he needed it for the auction. Alan convinced him to give him more time, that it wasn't finished. The other guy left and then…"

Nothing.

"Then?" Clay asked.

"Then…" She pushed her brain, trying to figure out what happened next. The blood pulsed behind her eyes and she blew out a low breath. "Oh my. I don't know what happened after that. I mean, I know—argh! This is so frustrating." Tears surfaced, surprising her. She swiped at them. "Sorry."

"Okay, stop," Toby said. "Just relax for a minute. It's coming back to you, but I don't think pushing for it helps."

She nodded. Then frowned. "What do you mean?"

"You're remembering, but it's coming in spurts when you don't expect it. So, just stop pressing yourself so hard."

He was right, but… Alan. "He didn't want to do it," she said. "I think he was buying time."

"What do you mean?"

She shook her head. "I don't know. I think Alan had the virus but didn't want to give it to the other man for some reason. He was buying time to do something on his own. I think. I don't know for sure, it's just a feeling I can't push away."

Clay rubbed his eyes. The man needed sleep and it

didn't appear to be on the agenda for him any time soon. "What if he had his own buyer?" he asked. "What if he needed time to get away and sell it and keep the money for himself?"

"What makes you say that?" Robin asked.

"One of the FBI agents working the case is a friend. I reached out to him and he agreed to keep me updated. This friend said they'd discovered that Alan Roberts had bought a round-trip plane ticket to Thailand leaving the next day. But what if he never planned to return? What if he planned to sell the virus that night and simply disappear?"

Robin swallowed hard. "Wow."

"Anything's possible at this point," Toby said. "I've called in reinforcements. My buddy, who also works with the FBI, Oliver Manning, is going to come help us out. I hope you don't mind that I asked."

"Of course not," Clay said. "I never turn down help."

The waitress delivered the food, and Robin's stomach turned. Her appetite had disappeared with the discovery that her coworker had developed a potentially deadly virus that could be used as a weapon should it fall into the wrong hands.

She forced herself to eat simply because she needed to stay strong, but her mind whirled in an endless spin. When she was finished eating, she placed the fork on the plate and continued to ponder the situation.

"Robin?"

She blinked and focused on Toby's concerned gaze.

"Did you remember something else?"

"No. Sorry."

"We're ready to go when you are."

"Of course." She followed Clay toward the exit with

Toby bringing up the rear. As they passed the large wall-sized window, it shattered.

A thousand needles pelted her left side before something slammed into her back and she fell hard to the floor.

ELEVEN

Toby rolled from Robin and reached for his weapon as the screams from the other diners washed over him. Bodies littered the floor, but at least they were moving. "Robin!"

"I'm okay." Her shaky voice reached him even as he turned to see for himself. Blood streaked the left side of her face. Clay and Trent were already outside the restaurant going after the shooter. Lance had positioned himself in front of Toby and Robin and shouted into his radio, requesting backup. Another round of bullets slammed into the restaurant.

"Everyone stay down!" Lance yelled.

Toby snagged Robin's hand. "Head for the back door by the bathrooms," he said. "Keep your head down and crawl."

She yanked her hand out of his grasp and slithered along the floor in a horrible army crawl, but it was getting the job done so he let her go. Toby stayed behind her.

A young woman lay on the floor hovering over her toddler who was strapped to her chest in a baby carrier. He touched her arm. "Come on," he said. "Stay with me."

Shaking, she nodded and crawled behind him while another bullet slammed into the counter. More screams echoed above the sirens.

Robin flinched and paused. Toby passed her and got to the bathroom door. He stood and pushed it open, then helped Robin and the young mother to their feet. "Stay against the wall. The shots are coming from the front so you should be safe here."

They obeyed without a word. Robin wrapped her arms around the sobbing mother and pulled her into a loose embrace while her gaze connected with Toby's. Everything in him wanted to turn and head back into the restaurant, but he didn't want to leave Robin unguarded.

Someone rounded the corner of the building and Toby lifted his weapon. "Freeze!" Then the uniform registered and he lowered the gun. "Lance."

"You okay?" Lance's concerned gaze took in Robin's bleeding face.

"Yeah," Toby said. "We're alive. Gotta get Robin to a doctor, but what about in there?"

"Trent and Clay went after the shooter. They think he was across the street behind the B&B. Clay told me to check on you two." He turned to the woman with the baby. "Brenda, James is waiting for you at the police station. I'll take you over there." Back to Toby. "Are you two going to be all right?"

"I've got it covered," Toby said. "If Trent and Clay are chasing the shooter, he's not aiming this way anymore."

"We've got cops from neighboring towns that are here and the two FBI agents jumped into the fray, as well. Guess that's one advantage to having them here." He shot them a tight smile and took Brenda's upper arm in a gentle grip. "Come on, let's get you and the baby to the station. James is worried sick." To Robin, he said, "Be sure you see Joshua soon. We've also got two ambulances out here and more on the way."

"Was anyone else hurt?" she asked.

"Looks like Ginger took a bullet to the upper shoulder and Harold had a graze across his forehead, but no one was killed."

"Oh, thank you," Robin breathed. She raised a shaky hand to shove stray hairs behind her ear.

Once Lance and Brenda were gone, Toby turned to Robin and she let out a breathy sob. He grasped her hands. "You've got some cuts on your face that need to be checked out."

He led her around the side of the building, keeping an eye on the surroundings. Clay and Trent may be after the shooter, but that didn't mean he couldn't double back in hopes of finishing the job.

But all was clear. Chaos to be sure, but no more bullets were flying. And Toby had managed to keep Robin from dying. Unlike the last time he'd been in a shootout with a woman he'd cared about. He put that memory into the back of his mind and concentrated on locating a paramedic who could take a look at Robin's face.

"This way," he said and led her to the closest ambulance. "Marcus, can you help us out?"

The young man turned and sized up the situation in the time it took to blink. He motioned to the back of the ambulance. "Let's see what we've got here."

Toby left Robin in the man's capable hands while he scanned the scene. The café's patrons were busy talking to officers, each other or getting medical care. And in the distance he saw a familiar face. Toby lifted a hand to snag the man's attention. "Oliver!"

The special agent paused, caught Toby's eye, then jogged over. Oliver clasped him in a man hug. "Toby, you're all right. I saw this craziness and had to make sure you were okay."

"We're fine. The café's going to need a lot of help, but thankfully no one was killed."

"Man, I can't believe this." Oliver shook his head and let his eyes rove the area in a manner very similar to what Toby had done just moments before. "It doesn't matter where it happens, it all looks the same."

"Yeah." He led Oliver to the back of the ambulance and winced when he saw Robin. The blood was gone, but the damage was visible. "Oliver, this is Robin. Robin, meet one of my best friends."

Oliver eyed the butterfly bandages on her cheeks and forehead. "That looks like it might be painful."

"It's from the glass that shattered with the first bullet," she said. "According to Marcus here, it's mostly superficial and no stitches needed. I'll heal. I'm just glad it didn't get me in the eyes."

"That would have been awful." Oliver turned to Toby. "Is there somewhere we can talk?"

"Yeah. We'll have to give a statement, but I'll get Clay to come to the B&B to get it." Toby glanced at Oliver. "Can you make sure it's safe to head over there?"

"Absolutely. I'll be right back." Oliver took off. Ten minutes later, he returned. "All looks quiet. He wasn't on the B&B property but the roof of the hardware store two doors down. You should be good to go."

"Thanks," Toby said. He turned to Robin. "Follow me." He kept a tight grip on her arm as he helped her out of the ambulance. "I'll see if Joshua can make a house call, as well."

"I don't need him to do that. I'll be fine. Sore, but fine."

"We'll see."

She jerked from his grip and shot him a glare. "I'm not a child."

Oliver raised a brow and stepped back. Toby felt the

heat grow from his toes to his ears in under a second. "I know you're not a child." He grimaced. "But I can see how it sounded like I was treating you like one. I'm sorry."

Robin's cheeks went pink. "No, I am. I'm touchy and grumpy."

"I'd say you have every right to be," Oliver murmured.

She sighed. "I'll see Joshua if I think I need to. Otherwise, let's get the statement done and see if I can press my brain into dredging up more memories."

Toby nodded, glad she had such a forgiving heart. Because the more memories she dredged up, the more forgiveness he was probably going to need.

Robin settled herself at the table with a bottle of water, a notepad and a pen. She wrote out everything she remembered about the shooting at the diner, which was mostly pain and fear. She'd never seen the shooter and doubted her statement would be much help, but within ten minutes, it was done and she was ready for some ibuprofen. Her cheek throbbed, the cuts along her jaw stung and her shoulder ached from Toby's tackle to the floor. At least her head wasn't pounding too awfully hard. She'd take her blessings where she could get them.

With a sigh, Robin pushed the paper to the middle of the table, debating what to do next. Leaving was an option, of course, but the people after her were more sophisticated than she'd originally given them credit for. Somehow, in spite of Toby and Amber's careful maneuvering, they'd been tracked to Wrangler's Corner.

She rubbed her eyes. The fire. She remembered it clearly now. And the arguing. She could hear the men yelling.

Pop, pop, pop.

She jerked straight up. Shooting? Had that been the

night of the fire or was she remembering the most recent incident?

Hands grabbing folders. She could see the hands. Definitely a man's hands and he'd stolen Alan's work.

Then turned—

A light rap on the door snapped her attention back to the present and she stood. Lance stepped into the kitchen followed by one of the FBI agents who'd been by yesterday. "Special Agent Young," she said. "What can I do for you?"

Lance cleared his throat. "He insisted on seeing you. But promised to leave if things get too…intense for you. Is that okay?"

"Yes, of course. Have a seat," she said.

Once Young was seated across from her, Lance crossed his arms. "If you need him to leave, just let me know. They've already agreed to give you some space and time so I'm not sure why he's here."

"It's okay, Lance, I can handle it." She hoped. But the truth was, as much as she appreciated Toby and everyone's help and determination to protect her, the resolution to his case—the lab explosion, the deaths of Alan Roberts and the other man, everything—rested with her.

"I'll explain," Young said.

"Go ahead." She briefly wondered if she should have Toby and Oliver sit in on the conversation in spite of her determination to be proactive going forward, but didn't want to disturb them if she didn't have to. She *could* do this.

He cleared his throat. "Thank you. And yes, Deputy Goode is correct. We agreed to let Toby work with you on remembering, but I wanted to make it clear that we have the best doctors at our disposal. If you'd be willing to talk to one of them, see if some of their techniques would work in helping you remember, we'd have one here ASAP."

Robin bit her lip. She hadn't considered going to see another doctor. Both the neurosurgeon and Joshua had seemed to think time, rest and healing would do it. Eventually. But because of the circumstances surrounding her amnesia, she supposed those investigating the explosion and murders wanted to speed things up a bit. And everything seemed to hinge upon her memory. "The person who killed Alan and the other man..."

Special Agent Young leaned forward. "Yes?"

"I think he stole some files. I remember the fire, the flames, the heat. And I remember seeing someone snatch a stack of files from Alan's workstation. I can see his hands, but I can't..." She sighed and shook her head. "I'm sorry, I just can't bring his face into focus."

"What's going on in here?" Toby asked from the doorway.

Robin gave him a tight smile, irritated at his interruption. "I'm just trying to remember." She spotted Oliver standing behind Toby's right shoulder.

Toby's frosty glare settled on Special Agent Young. "I thought we had an agreement."

"We did, but we need answers, Toby." He raked a hand through his dark hair. "We've got a big bunch of nothing including a dead guy that could have been our biggest lead. And then there's the guy who keeps trying to kill Robin." He narrowed his gaze. "You know as well as I do that the sooner she remembers, the sooner she's safe."

"I want her to remember. I just don't want her pressured to the point that it's so stressful you do more harm than good."

Special Agent Young sighed. "I don't want that either. That's why I'm recommending the doctors."

"No," Robin said. Everyone in the kitchen went still. "I appreciate everyone's concern, but the fact is I'm re-

membering more every day. I think if you just let me do
this on my own, I will. If your doctors come here, there's
a chance they could be shot at or blown up or...or...*something*. I'm a little dangerous to be around these days." Her
frustration rang clear, and the men looked at one another.

Special Agent Young rubbed his eyes. "Look, can you
just start at the beg—"

"No," Oliver said as he stepped around Toby and into
the kitchen. "Toby's right. Don't push her."

The agent's jaw tightened. "What are you doing here,
Manning?"

"Same thing you are. Just in a more unofficial capacity. Ben was my friend, too."

"This is our case now." The special agent stood. "Leave
it alone."

Oliver shrugged. "Leave *her* alone. For now."

"Excuse me," Robin bit out. She stood. "I think everyone needs to stop trying to decide what's best for me and
let *me* decide that." Her words snapped through the air and
silence reigned. "Thank you. Now." She turned her attention to Special Agent Young. "I'll consider seeing one of
the doctors. Give me a little time to think about it. It's not
a bad idea, and I promise to consider it."

Young pursed his lips, then stood. "All right. Thank
you for thinking about it." He hesitated. "Will you at least
keep me updated on what you're remembering?"

"Of course."

Young nodded and slipped out the door.

"So," Robin said, "what do you guys want for dinner?"

Toby blinked, then chuckled. "I think we'll let you decide that."

She rolled her eyes. "I've decided that you can have
some input."

"What are the options?"

Robin opened the freezer. "Wow. It's well stocked. I'd say chicken or some kind of casserole. There's also a beef stew and rice with a side of garlic bread. What suits you?"

Toby shut the freezer and gently guided her out of the kitchen, down the hall and to her bedroom. He opened the door and motioned for her to enter. She did and turned to face him. "What?"

"Look, Robin, I appreciate your desire to do everything you can to remember. I also appreciate the fact that you want to take charge of your situation and the fact you have this never-quit attitude, but you're hurt. You've been bombed out of your lab, smoked out of your home, chased through the woods, shot at while trying to enjoy a simple meal and grilled by an FBI agent."

"He was actually very pleasant."

"Good, I'm glad, but you need to heal. Now, I don't want to do anything that's going to seem like I'm treating you like a child—"

"Like sending me to my room?"

He dropped his head for a moment, then heaved a sigh. "I'm not sending you to your room. I'm simply suggesting that you need some time to recover. Today was traumatic and scary and…hard. On everyone."

At his compassion, his gentle caring, the walls around her heart cracked, and the wall holding back her fear and tears crumbled to dust. "It was scary," she whispered. "It was awful." Tears tracked her cheeks, and he pulled her against him and rested his chin on the top of her head.

"I'm sorry," he said. "I thought it would be okay to go there with all of us surrounding you, that there would be safety in numbers. I thought I could keep you safe."

"It's not your fault," she said. "It's not anyone's fault but the person trying to kill me. And you did keep me safe. And other people there, too. But…"

"But what?"

"I can't put other people in danger. I think today was a clear example that I have to stay under the radar and hide away from the innocents who might wind up being collateral damage until this is over."

"I agree."

She nodded against his shoulder. Fatigue pulled at her. Her heart pounded at the comfort she drew from being in his arms before a memory shattered her calm.

How could you?

Robin stilled as she recalled the words she'd thrown at the man holding her. *How could you do this? I thought you were my friend!*

A gasp slipped from her. "Did we have an argument?"

He tensed and dropped his arms to cup her elbows. "What makes you ask that?"

"I'm not sure. I just had a memory of me yelling at you."

Toby frowned. "Yelling what?"

"I wanted to know how you could do…something. And that I thought you were my friend. What did I mean by that? What were we arguing about?"

Toby closed his eyes and quickly ran through a variety of answers that he could give her that wouldn't be outright lies. "Yes, we argued."

"About?"

"I… I want to tell you, but I can't."

"Why not?"

"Because I think you should remember it on your own. If I nudge your memories, you may think you remember something, but you don't really. You'll be influenced by what I tell you."

"But if I was mad at you about something, I think I should know what."

Toby cupped her chin and stared into the eyes that he was already halfway in love with. He refused to lie to her. Simply didn't have it in him. "Yes. I think you should, too, but I also think we should just give your mind some more time to remember on its own."

If he told her now, she'd push him away faster than he could blink and then be at the mercy of the two agents—and a killer. "Look, I promise that I have nothing but your best interests at heart. I want to protect you. I want to put an end to all the craziness, but I just don't want to tell you right now."

She frowned and swiped a tear from her cheek as she searched his eyes. "I'm not sure I like that, but okay. I guess. Because I trust you."

Those last four words pierced his heart, and his guilt flooded him. It was all Toby could do not to blurt out the truth and get on his knees to beg her forgiveness. But that would come in time. If she even gave him a chance to beg. "Please, Robin, just rest. You might even wake up and re-member the argument. If you do, come to me and we'll talk about it." He gave a light shrug. "All friends argue every once in a while."

It was the truth. And it was the best he could come up with without flat-out lying to her.

She sighed and pressed a hand to her head. "I think you're right. I need to lie down."

"Go. Let me handle this."

She started to turn, then spun back to face him. "Why?" she whispered. "Why does it matter so much to you? Why are you putting yourself—your life—on the line for me? You could just dump me somewhere or let the FBI agents haul me off to question me. But you're stepping into the gap for me. Not that I don't appreciate it because I do. Very much. But why?"

Toby paused. Connected his gaze with hers—and, again, frantically searched for an answer that wasn't a lie. "Before the explosion, we were friends, Robin. Good friends. Honestly, everything I'm doing is simply because I care about you. Bottom line is I want you safe, and I'll do whatever it takes to make sure that happens. You don't deserve any of this. And…"

"And?"

"I failed once to keep someone I cared about safe. I don't want to fail again," he said softly.

She blinked. "What do you mean, you failed?"

He hesitated, then nodded to the sitting room at the end of the hall. "This may take a few minutes. You want to hear it now or lie down for a while first?"

"Now. Please."

Once they were seated, he cleared his throat. "Oliver and I have been friends for a long time. He was married to Debra. At some point during their marriage, Debra started accusing him of cheating on her."

She winced. "Was he?"

"No. Not at all." He swiped a hand over his face, hating the memories of that day, but Robin deserved to know. Truthfully, she deserved to know everything he could tell her—including their past relationship. And he'd tell her if he didn't think she would shut him out of her life and leave herself an easy target for the killer after her. So for now, he'd tell her what he could.

His mind went back to that time of sorrow and grief and he wished he could change the past. Or forget it. Some days he thought he'd welcome a case of amnesia himself. Remembering hurt.

"Oliver used to do a lot of undercover stuff," he said. "Debra called me to their house one morning, crying, yelling that she couldn't get ahold of Oliver. I couldn't either, but I knew he was working on a case so I went over and tried to calm her down. She was behaving so out of character that it scared me. I worked hard to convince Deb that he was working, not meeting anyone and that he would be home later to talk to her. But she wasn't buying it. She wanted to know where he was."

"Did you tell her?"

"I couldn't. At that point, I didn't know where he was either, but I told her I was meeting him later that afternoon and would tell him to get in touch with her."

Robin frowned. "She didn't know what he did for a living?"

"Of course. Well, not until after they were married, but yes."

"Wait a minute. He didn't tell her until after they were married that he did undercover gigs?"

"Yeah."

She let out a low breath. "Wow. That's really wrong."

He raked a hand through his hair. "I agree. But there's more to it than that."

"What?"

He had to tell her. To take a chance and pray she didn't remember the email just yet. "Ben, Oliver and I used to work with the CIA."

Robin gaped. He let her process, searching her gaze for any sign that the CIA reference triggered memories of the email. Finally, she said, "You?"

"Yes."

"Were you working for the CIA while at the university?"

"No." She didn't remember the email. He blew out a low breath of relief. "I quit about two years ago after Debra died. While teaching, I was just that. A teacher.

Trying to live a normal life and leave all the espionage behind."

"Oh."

"After an…incident… Oliver went over to the FBI about the time I quit and convinced Ben to go with him. He tried to recruit me, too, but I was still dealing with something and decided I wasn't ready to return to any form of law enforcement. That's when I started teaching full-time."

Her frown deepened. "What was the incident?"

Toby stared at his clasped hands. What could it hurt to tell her? Other than the fact that it might jog her memory about the email. But if mentioning he'd been with the CIA hadn't done it, maybe this wouldn't either. Studying her narrowed eyes, he decided he was going to have to chance it. She was already perturbed that he wouldn't tell her about the argument.

"Oliver and I had learned about a potential foreign threat and were looking into it. We were set to meet a man we'd been after for a while. This guy had a lot of suspicious overseas banking activity going on, and we finally managed to get a meeting with him. Under the guise of being buyers."

"Okay," she said.

"I was at Debra's house trying to calm her down, but time was running out and I had to leave to make the meeting. Only I didn't want to leave Debra alone in that emotional state. I called her best friend and had her come over to stay with her. But…" Reliving that day had his head pounding. "Apparently, Debra didn't believe me when I told her Oliver wasn't cheating on her," he said, "and she ditched her friend and followed me."

He shook his head and steeled his heart against the horror of that day. "She…ah…drove up just as one of our assets was talking to Oliver. He laughed at something she said and she reached out to touch his hand. A completely innocent gesture, but Debra launched out of her car and started yelling at Oliver—screeching at him that she was sick and tired of him and his lies and she was done with him and his covert life. One of the men opened fire. We scattered, but it was too late. Deb was dead. The first bullet went right through her heart and killed her instantly."

Tears shimmered on Robin's lashes and she blew out a low breath. "Oh, Toby. How awful."

"It was. We managed to get what we needed to neutralize the threat and put a lot of people behind bars, but it didn't matter. Debra was dead, and Oliver was...shattered."

"And you blamed yourself."

He swallowed and looked away. "I never considered she would follow me. I kept only half an eye out for a tail but wasn't really concerned about someone following me. I was more concerned—more focused—about what we were going to be walking in to."

"That's understandable."

"No. Not really. I knew she was upset. Very upset, but she seemed to have calmed down before I had to leave, and her friend was there. I never expected Debra to do that."

"It wasn't your fault."

He sighed. "I feel like it was. Regardless, Oliver later told me they'd been having problems for a while and were seeing a counselor."

"I'm so sorry."

"So...yeah. After that, I just lost my focus and needed something different."

"And that's when you decided to teach?"

He nodded. "Part of my cover as an operative was being a university professor so the credentials were legit. When

I quit the CIA, I put them to good use—for real that time. And that's how I met you."

She palmed her eyes. "I want to remember," she whispered.

"You will, Robin," he said. Sadness gripped him. "You will."

TWELVE

Robin kicked the covers off and rolled to look at the clock. Two o'clock in the morning. She squinted in the darkness, wondering what woke her. Her head ached, of course, but it was probably a three on a scale of one to ten.

She slipped out of bed and padded to the door to look out into the hall. On any other night, the night-light would have made the area feel soft and homey, cozy. Tonight, the shadows dancing on the ceiling and walls sent chills down her spine and goose bumps pebbling over her skin.

The silence slid over her. She wanted to call out to Toby or one of the others, but something held her quiet. Where were the two officers from Nashville Clay had recruited to help out?

After Toby had told her his past history with Oliver and Debra, she'd been wiped out, emotionally and physically. She'd fallen into bed, waking just a few minutes ago because she heard something—or thought she did.

A sound came from the kitchen. A footstep? It had to be one of the deputies or Toby. Didn't it? Instead of returning to his sister's cottage, Toby had decided to stay in the room off the kitchen that held two sets of bunk beds. The men had agreed to take shifts monitoring the house and the surrounding area and sleeping.

If an intruder had gotten in, surely Toby would have warned her. Unless he was hurt. But what about the others? Asleep? Rattled, she couldn't remember the rotation schedule. On silent feet, she headed for the kitchen.

A shadow moved to her right, and she squelched the scream that rose. Barely. "Toby," she whispered. He placed a finger on his lips, and she pressed a hand to her racing heart. "What is it?" she whispered.

"Not sure," he said, his voice so low she had to strain to hear it. "Stay behind me."

She did as he said and placed her hands on his waist. He moved down the hallway, so quiet she wouldn't have known he was there if she hadn't been touching him.

At the end, he stopped and peered around the doorjamb into the kitchen, then pulled back. Without speaking, he motioned for her to stay put. With his weapon held ready, he hooked around the doorjamb and into the room. "Hands in the air!"

A curse rang out. The back door slammed open, and running footsteps pounded down the steps.

"I'm going after him! Stay here and lock the door!" Toby didn't slow as he yelled the words over his left shoulder.

Another figure burst from the cruiser across the street and joined Toby in pursuit. Yet another officer approached from the other direction and hurried up the stairs to join her in the kitchen. Officer Paul Sanchez. She'd met him last night when Clay had been here to introduce them as friends he used to work with in Nashville.

"You need to go with them," she said.

"They'll be all right. If that was a diversion to get you alone in the house, we don't want it to work, right?"

"Oh. Right." She shivered, the chill in her bones due to more than the temperature outside. Officer Sanchez turned the coffee machine on and popped a coffee pod into the top.

Robin clasped her hands and strode into the den to flip the switch next to the fireplace. The gas logs sprang to life and soon, heat blew out of the vent, warming her. She was attempting to thaw the cold knot of fear that had formed in her belly. But she didn't think that would happen until she knew Toby and the others were safe.

Officer Sanchez walked over and pressed a warm mug of liquid into her hands and she took a sip. "Thank you."

"Sometimes it's easier to warm up from the inside out."

"Yeah." She took another sip. "Will they call if they catch him?"

"I'm sure they'll let us know as soon as possible."

"Good." She paced to the window, stood to the side and looked out. The darkness covered the town—and just like earlier, what should have been a comforting, soothing sight now seemed eerie. Even sinister. The chill returned, popping goose bumps along her spine. She sent up prayers for Toby and the other officer's safety and that finally, the killer would be caught.

Toby pulled to a stop outside the door of the empty building with the For Lease sign in the window. The intruder from the B&B had ducked inside and slammed the door shut. Yelling at him to stop had proved useless. Officer George Baxter from Nashville pulled up the rear. "Cover the back," Toby said.

"I've got Clay on the radio," George said. "He's on his way with more backup." George sprinted to the end of the building and disappeared around the side.

Toby wasn't waiting on backup. He wanted this guy now. He twisted the knob and stepped inside, weapon drawn, adrenaline pumping. The building had once been a convenience store with metal shelves set up in rows from front to back. He'd have to clear it by himself. Toby eased to the first row and darted a peek around the edge.

Clear.

The second, third and fourth rows were also clear.

Heart still thumping triple time, he bolted toward the restrooms. Quickly, he cleared each one, then the storage room and office.

In the office, he found a set of stairs that led up. "Great," he whispered. Into the radio, he said, "Going up to the roof."

Step by step, he climbed, wincing with each creak of the old wood, expecting someone to appear at the top and shoot him. He'd be an easy target, trapped on the stairs between the wooden walls. Sweat rolled down his temples and dripped from his chin. Finally, at the top, with his weapon in front of him, he stepped into another storage area. An attic.

A gust of cold wind blasted his face, and he hurried to the open window straight ahead. Carefully, he stuck his head out. Looked up. Down. And there the man went, skittering down the fire escape.

"Stop!" Toby called.

The guy never paused. Why did he bother to yell?

Toby swung out of the window and began the descent. "He's on the fire escape," he said into the radio. "Stop him!"

But instead of heading for the street, the figure bolted toward the back alley, scampered up the chain-link fence and vaulted to the ground. Toby followed, but by the time he was on the other side of the fence, the guy was gone.

He gave his location into the radio and hurried after the intruder without much hope of finding him. A multitude of streets led to alleys and business. All of which would provide excellent hiding places. The screech of rubber on asphalt reached him and the wink of taillights disappeared around the next corner.

Toby called it in. "He's on Round Rock Way traveling north. Make and model of the vehicle unknown."

The fence rattled behind him and Toby spun to see George drop over and land feetfirst. He jogged over to Toby. "Got away?"

"Yeah. He had a car waiting."

"He knows this place."

Toby shook his head. "He had his escape route planned before he even showed up in the house."

"So, what was the purpose in that?"

"I don't know. Unless he planned to grab Robin and force her to go with him."

George shook his head. "He had to know about the security."

"Yeah. And because he knew, he was able to get past it. That worries me."

"Had to be an inside job. He got his information from someone."

"Exactly, but who?" Toby asked. "I can't imagine anyone I know or work with being involved."

"No idea, but I recommend making a list and checking it twice this season. Because someone's not being very nice these days."

"No kidding." Toby slapped a hand against his thigh and looked at the fence. "It's going to be harder to get back over now that the adrenaline rush has faded."

George laughed. "Come on, old man, I'll give you a boost."

Toby shot the guy a tight smile, walked to the gate and unlatched it. "I think I'll use this, but feel free to do it your way."

George followed him through the gate while checking in with Clay on the status of the intruder. He hung up. "They lost him," George said. "Actually, they never saw him."

Lips tight, Toby nodded. "I'm not surprised. Not with as well as he had this all planned out."

The bed-and-breakfast was lit up brighter than the Christmas tree on the front porch. Toby rapped on the door and was glad to see Robin hanging back while Paul opened it. When she saw it was him, she rushed to him and wrapped her arms around his waist. "I'm so glad you're okay," she said.

Her concern gripped his heart in a way that had him pulling her into a hug. "I'm fine, Robin. I'm just glad you're okay."

"Me? I wasn't the one chasing a possible killer." She stepped back and ran her fingers through her hair, mussing it in a way that he found endearing. His fingers itched to replace hers. Instead, he cleared his throat and ordered himself to focus.

"Why would he break in like that when it's obvious this place has security inside and out?" she asked. "Why take a chance on getting caught?"

"Because getting to you is apparently worth the risk," George said.

Toby frowned at the man, but Robin didn't seem fazed. "This is crazy," she muttered.

"Or," Toby said, "maybe he was just trying to see how hard it would be to breach the security around here."

"Didn't seem to be that difficult," Paul said. "Sorry about that, Robin."

"It's not your fault," she said.

"Of course it is. It's a collective fault. He never should have made it into the house."

"He's right," Toby said. "Of course, it would help if this place had an alarm system we could arm, but people are coming and going at all hours. There's no way Sabrina could turn it on if she had one."

"I thought about that," Paul said, "but figured with all of us here, it wouldn't matter that much."

"Please, everyone stop beating yourselves up. I'm still here, he's gone, and everything is fine. For now."

A knock on the door stilled them for a brief second. Toby turned to peer out the window. "It's Oliver." He opened the door to find his friend with his hand on his weapon.

"Everything okay over here?"

"It is right now. How'd you know something was going on?"

"I was out walking." Oliver frowned. "You know my sleep habits."

Toby did. They were practically nonexistent since his wife's murder. "Come on in."

"Hold up," Clay said from behind Oliver, "I'm here, too."

Oliver stepped into the foyer and shed his coat. He hung it on the antique rack to his right and rubbed his hands together. "Forgot my gloves. I saw all the commotion and thought I'd check in with you."

Clay didn't bother to remove his coat.

"We had an intruder," Toby told Oliver and led him and Clay into the den to join the others.

"He got in the house?" Oliver asked.

"Yes." Toby clipped off the word and sank onto the sofa next to Robin.

"How? Where was everyone?"

"Not sure. I was sleeping when I heard someone in the kitchen. Paul was walking the perimeter, and George was watching the front door from the cruiser. Clay, Lance and Trent had gone home to get some sleep."

"What about the alarm system?" Oliver asked.

"There's not one," Toby said, then looked at Robin. "I think we're going to have to move again."

Robin's shoulders dipped. "Where? The jail?"

Toby raised a brow. "Actually, that's not a bad idea."

Robin gaped. "I was just kidding."

Oliver rubbed his chin. "I have a better idea. What if we ask the two special agents who're in town to join forces and add their protection expertise to this place?"

"I don't know if I want them anywhere near Robin right now," Toby said with a deep scowl. "Agent Young overstepped in pushing her to remember. I don't trust him not to do it again."

"Toby..." Robin said, brows dipped. "He didn't overstep. He's just trying to help."

"I'll rein them in," Oliver said, "but come on, Toby, you know as well as I do that this is a good setup even without the alarm system. You're right down the street from the police station. The diner across the street is open, and people are walking the sidewalks at all hours."

"I get that, but it didn't make much of a difference tonight, did it? Someone still got *in* the house."

"How?"

The room fell silent. Then Toby gave a disgusted sigh. "I don't know. We were so focused on catching the guy and making sure Robin was safe, we haven't stopped to figure it out yet."

"Then figure it out and plug the hole."

"Yeah." Paul stood. "I've got the windows down here."

"I'll check upstairs," George said.

Toby reached for Robin's hand. "I'll stay with Robin."

Clay rubbed his chin. "I'm going to tape off the perimeter of the house until we can take a look in the morning. If someone was snooping around outside earlier, there could be prints. We'll rule out Paul and George's shoe prints and see what's left. If anything."

The others went to work leaving Toby, Robin and Oliver in the den. Robin drew in a deep breath and pressed a hand to her suddenly pounding head. "I think Oliver might be right," she said.

"How so?" Toby rubbed her cold hands between his warm ones, and she closed her eyes at the comfort the gesture brought.

"That I should stay here," she said. "If I leave, he's just going to follow. And besides, where would I go?"

"A safe house," Tby said.

"Sounds like an oxymoron in my case," she muttered.

A sigh slipped from Toby. "Aw, Robin, we're going to get to the bottom of this."

She bit her lip and looked away. His sweet kindness would have her blubbering once again if she wasn't careful. She stood. "Thank you. And now, I'm going to go back to bed and try to sleep." The sun would be coming up in a couple of hours, and even if she found she couldn't sleep, she could think.

Once she was settled back in her bed, she lay still, listening. And realized she'd left before finding out how the intruder had entered the house. Did it matter? As long as the people guarding her knew, she didn't need to, did she?

Of course she did. With a sigh, she swung her legs over the side of the bed, dressed and headed to the kitchen since that seemed to be the place everyone congregated.

As she drew close, voices reached her. Toby and Oliver. "…think about her every day, Toby."

"I know."

"She shouldn't have been there."

"I know that, too. I can't apologize enough." A pause. "I'm sorry I pulled away, Oliver. I shouldn't have. I just… every time I saw you, I relived it. But…that was selfish and I'm sorry."

"Don't be. It wasn't your fault, it was *mine*. Don't you get it? I should have had someone with her. I should have noticed how far she'd deteriorated. But it was so *fast*—"

The men fell silent, and part of Robin wanted to stay and listen. The other part of her said she needed to leave, that the conversation wasn't any of her business. She started to return to her room when she heard Toby finally say, "If I could go back and change that day, I would, but I can't. And I can't keep living in the past either."

A heavy sigh escaped one of them. She thought it was Oliver. "Some days I can't find the strength to live anywhere else," the special agent said in a low voice. Then cleared his throat and sniffed.

Robin ached for the two of them. They'd suffered so much. And she didn't need to keep standing there, but she really wanted to know how the person got in. She tiptoed backward and then approached the kitchen at a slow pace, clearing her throat to give them a heads-up.

When she entered, Toby frowned. "Can't sleep?"

"Haven't really tried yet. I kept thinking about the intruder. Did you figure out how he got in?"

"Through a second-story balcony window," Oliver said. "He cut the glass and simply reached in and unlocked the door."

"How did he get up there without anyone seeing him?"

"The trellis on the side of the carport," Toby said. "He climbed up and walked across the roof, then lowered himself to the second-floor balcony. Cut the glass, opened the door and made himself at home." He shook his head. "I noticed the trellis but didn't want to request that it be removed since it would be such an invasion. I should have. Instead, I just requested Robin have a first-floor room closest to the kitchen."

"Were the guys doing predictable perimeter checks?" Oliver asked.

"No, they were supposed to be intermittent."

Oliver shrugged. "Well, doesn't really matter. All he had to do was wait him out and as soon as the officer was out of sight, haul himself up the trellis and onto the roof. Easy peasy."

Toby grimaced, and Robin felt sorry for him. He was blaming himself for a lot of things that he shouldn't. "I think the fact that my room was on the bottom floor is what saved me, Toby, so don't beat yourself up. The intruder might have thought I was on the second floor and that's why he entered that way."

"No," Toby said, "that was just the only way he could have gotten in without being detected." He rubbed his chin. "And now that we know about it, we'll take precautions." He nodded. "I think staying here is going to work out. Now that our intruder knows we know how he got in, he also knows we'll be a lot more vigilant. I'll be surprised if he makes another attempt here at the house. At least any time soon."

"So, he'll wait for me to leave the house to strike."

"Probably."

She nodded and bit her lip. "All right. Then let's set something up so he'll come after me. But it has to be something that won't endanger others."

"No way," Toby said. "That has disaster written all over it."

Anger with him flared. She did her best to bite it back. "Not if you're there to make sure nothing goes wrong."

He shook his head. "Something always goes wrong."

I can't believe you would do this! You used me!

A flash of rage took her by surprise and she swallowed, wondering at the anger—where it had come from and unsure what to do with it. "Are you letting one incident from your past influence this decision?" She slapped a hand over her mouth, appalled the words had spilled out.

Toby went still. So very still. Oliver drew in a quick breath and Robin blinked. Just as quickly, the anger, the hurt were gone—and remorse took over.

Toby blew out a slow breath. "No, I'm not. What's influencing that decision is the fact that it's dangerous and, just like the trellis thing, there's no surefire way to make sure you won't be hurt in the process."

"I see. But what if I want to do it?" she asked, placing her hands on her hips and jutting her chin.

He bit his lip. Probably remembering her order not to treat her like a child. She appreciated his attempt to filter his words. He finally nodded. "All right. What if we see if we can come up with an alternate plan to draw the killer out? And if we can't, then we'll consider your idea."

Grateful neither man addressed her stubbornness, she harrumphed—this time without any anger or messy emotions—and crossed her arms. "You expect to come up with a better plan and are just humoring me, aren't you?"

"Yes."

A giggle escaped, surprising her as well as the two men. She covered her mouth. "Sorry. That just slipped out. I'm so tired I'm giddy, I think." And the wide swing of emotions scared her. She'd remembered part of their argument and needed to process it. Tears surfaced, and she turned to go.

Toby caught her hand and pulled her against him. She drew in his scent and simply let herself feel safe for a brief moment. Then she pulled away. She *wasn't* safe, and the people trying to help her weren't either. The only way to ensure their safety was for her to remember.

THIRTEEN

At breakfast the next morning, Toby sat at the table waiting for Oliver, who said he had some information he needed to give Toby. While he waited, he thought about the conclusion he'd come to last night and the fact that he was going to have to help Robin remember. Somehow. He wasn't trained in that kind of thing, but he could give her access to people who were.

Caught between a rock and a hard place didn't come close to how he was feeling. Once she remembered, they'd be able to catch the person responsible. And Robin would be safe. And she would remember the email, as well as why she didn't want anything more to do with him. And he would be out of her life once more.

Assuming they were even *able* to help her.

It was a moot point if they couldn't. He dropped his head in his hands. All he wanted was what was best for Robin and to catch whoever was responsible for all of the chaos. Maybe it was time to man up and tell her exactly what they'd been fighting about and see if that jogged her memory. If she sent him away, then he would just have to find a way to protect her from a distance. And he knew Clay wouldn't allow anything to happen to her.

So, to tell or not to tell?

Robin entered the kitchen, grabbed a cup of coffee and a bagel and settled into the chair next to him at the table. "Good morning. Were you up all night? Or did you get some sleep?" she asked.

"I managed to snag a few hours. How about you?"

She shrugged and reached for a knife and a tub of cream cheese. "It was restless, but I think I slept. Any more news about the intruder from last night?"

"Clay went out at first light and checked the footprints. He took two casts of prints that looked like they might be different from Greg's and Paul's shoes, so we'll see what he comes up with. Said the person was probably about five-ten with a size eleven shoe."

"Well, we can hope that will help whenever we have a suspect to match it to."

"It's helped crack cases before. Maybe this time will be the same."

"While I don't mind small talk," she said. "I have a feeling that you want to say something more." She took a bite of the bagel and chewed while her eyes never left his.

He smiled. "Nothing gets past you, does it?"

"Talk to me, Toby."

He blew out a sigh. "All right. I haven't been entirely forthcoming about everything."

She took another bite of the bagel and studied him. "I know."

"While I would rather you remember everything on your own, I think maybe it's time to talk about some things."

"Like what?"

He glanced at the clock. Did he have time for this? "Like the fact that we spent a lot of time together and I was…developing feelings for you."

"What kind of feelings?" she asked softly.

"Feelings I couldn't act on because—"

A knock on the door shut off his words, and Toby let out a groan, barely resisting the urge to bang his head on the table.

Robin blinked. "Who's that?"

"Oliver. He said he was going to come by. He said he had some information he needed to share with us." He paused. "Can we continue this after he leaves?"

"Of course."

Toby let Oliver in, and he took a seat at the kitchen table after helping himself to a blueberry bagel.

"What's the information?" Toby asked.

"Agent Young shared some security footage from the night of the explosion. He wanted to come over and ask Robin to take a look, but I told him it might be better if I handled it. Honestly, I'm not sure what he thinks Robin will be able to tell him, but he wouldn't take no for an answer."

Robin leaned forward. "Let me see."

The agent pulled his phone from the clip on his belt and tapped the screen. "The lab is right across from the student building. One of the security cameras picked up someone running from the blaze, but I don't see how you'll be able to identify him because there's tons of smoke and he has a hood over his head." He turned the phone so that she and Toby could see it. Toby tapped play, and the video began to play.

The picture was surprisingly good and opened with the explosion. Unfortunately, the camera from the student center was aimed at the front of the building, and the initial explosion took place toward the back. Therefore, the only thing one could see was the smoke billowing from the back.

"The person who chased me," Robin said, "would have left the building through the front door, most likely."

Toby paused the video. "How do you know that?"

Robin gaped. "I don't know. I… That just came out. I had a brief picture of me running through the lab toward the bathrooms. They're at the front, right?"

"Yes. You broke a window in the men's bathroom at the front of the building. That's how you escaped, remember?"

"No, not really." She frowned. "Actually, maybe I do, a little." Her eyes widened. "I remember. I ran into the bathroom, and then there was another explosion. The door flew in…"

"And?"

"Pain," she whispered, touching her forehead. "It hurt." She pinched the bridge of her nose. "It's so weird. They're memories, but they're not. It's like I'm watching snippets of a movie with a bad reel. Some parts are skipped, others are perfectly clear."

"It's okay, Robin," Toby said. "Try not to get frustrated."

She scowled but nodded.

"So, the person who killed the other two scientists would have chased you toward the front," Oliver said. "If you locked yourself in the bathroom, the guy probably figured you were trapped with no way out. The fire would have been spreading quickly and he would've had to get out before he was trapped, too."

"But someone saw me break the window and escape," Robin said, "and that's why they want to get rid of me."

"Yes."

"There's someone at the top calling the shots," she said. "All of these attempts on my life are made by different people. How many goons does the guy have on his payroll?"

"Apparently plenty," Toby muttered. He pressed the play button, and the video continued. The front door of the lab swung open and a figure darted out and soon disappeared from view out of range of the camera. Then another explosion sent flames shooting out the front.

Toby rewound the footage and pressed Pause at the point where the person bolted out of the door. "He has something in his hands. Can we zoom in on that?"

"Something in his hands?" Oliver frowned.

"Yeah." Toby zoomed the video.

"Files," Robin said. "He took the files from the desk."

Oliver stiffened. "Are you sure?"

"Yes."

"Who?"

She shook her head. "I don't know. I can't see his face, just a brief picture of his hands sweeping the files from the desk. And then nothing." She sighed.

Oliver stood. "I'll get this sent to Quantico and see if someone can enlarge it."

"What for?" Robin asked.

The agent shrugged. "You never know what they'll be able to pull off of it." He stood. "I'll see myself out. Take care of yourself, Robin. And watch your back."

Toby slid an arm around her shoulders. "That's what I'm here for."

Once Oliver was gone, Toby led her into the den. He sat next to her on the sofa and she struggled not to notice how much his presence affected her, how safe he made her feel—and how his words continued to echo through her thoughts.

His admission that his feelings for her had been *developing* made her want to smile in spite of her circumstances because each day, she found herself drawn more and more to the mysterious man. And yet…

Her smile faded. He was still hiding something from her.

"You're remembering more every day," he said.

"I am. But the bits and pieces and little snatches of memory here and there…" She shook her head. "It's driving me crazy."

"I'm sure."

She fell silent. "Those folders that the killer grabbed. What do you think they contain that was worth killing for?"

"I think you know as well as I do."

She sighed. "The instructions on how to make the virus?"

"I'd say it's highly likely."

"He can't do anything with the information unless he has someone who can interpret it for him—and I'm not even sure he has it all. That piece of paper only had part of the information. A lot of it, yes, but not all of it."

"You figured it out easy enough."

"But it was just one possibility. It might not even be what Alan came up with."

Toby shrugged. "Regardless, I don't think it will be hard to find someone willing to recreate it for the right price. And as soon as he knows the coast is clear, he'll start putting out feelers for that person. That is, if he doesn't already have someone."

"Coast is clear," she said. "Meaning when I'm dead?"

"Yeah. But that's not going to happen."

"I hope not. I mean, who could have been in the lab that night besides those of us who worked there?" she asked. "That's what I keep coming back to. I knew everyone who worked there, right?"

"Of course."

"So, who knew what Alan was working on and would be meeting that night?"

"I know the investigators are looking at all of the employees, questioning their whereabouts and whether they saw anything. They're also viewing all of the security video they can get their hands on, trying to see who was on campus that night, who was going in and out of the lab, and so on, but so far, I've heard nothing." He paused. "Of course, Ben was the one keeping me in the loop."

"Well, now you have Oliver."

"Yes."

"Do you think they'll find anything, though?"

He shrugged. "You never know. Sure can't hurt to try." His phone buzzed, and he glanced at the screen and frowned.

"What is it?" she asked.

"One of the FBI agents. Either Young or McBride." He answered. "Hello?" A pause. "Yes." He sighed and rubbed his eyes. "Fine. No, I'll come to you. What room? Give me a few minutes to make sure everything's okay here and I'll be over."

She lifted a brow. "Be over where?"

"Agent McBride said they had a few more questions for me. I'll go over there. I don't want them bothering you. Lance and Trent will be on guard."

"Toby, it's okay if they come over here."

He hesitated. "Honestly, I'm not sure if they really do have questions or if this is just an attempt to come over here to press you some more."

"I can handle it, Toby."

He paused. "I don't doubt you can, I just don't know that you should have to." A frown creased his brow. "But if you want them to come over here, I'll call McBride back and tell them to."

Did she really want to do that? No. And besides, what could she tell them that they didn't already know? "It's okay. Go talk to them and if you think I can add anything to the conversation, bring them over."

Toby gave a short nod. "All right, that's the way we'll play it then."

He let Trent and Lance in on the plan, then took her hand. "Hang in there, Robin. Hopefully, all of this is just for a little while longer. You've got my number. Call me if you need anything. I'm going to let Oliver know what's going on and maybe he can help keep an eye on the place, too. I'm just a few minutes away, okay?"

"I'll be fine, Toby. Go."

He pulled her into a hug, then kissed her—a comforting, if slightly desperate, meeting of the lips that sent Robin's heart pounding. Before he could pull away she wound her arms around his neck and held on, kissing him back, trying to put all of her emotions into the moment.

He lifted his head, the longing in his eyes making her palms sweat. He walked backward to the door. "I wasn't going to do that."

"But you did."

"I did." He grabbed his coat and hat from the hook by the door and pulled them on. "I'm falling for you, Robin, and I can't."

"Why not?" She didn't recognize her own voice. Breathless and thin.

"Because it's complicated."

"Complicated. Well, what isn't these days?" She sighed. "Go, we'll talk later."

"Yes, we're going to have to." And then he was heading out the door, his phone out, Oliver on the line.

Robin pressed shaky fingers to her lips and closed her eyes. "Complicated," she muttered. "No kidding." What was she not remembering? "Come on, brain, fill in the blanks." The fire. The smoke. The fear. Yes, she remembered all that.

Pop.

And just like that, the memory was there. She saw Alan jerk as the bullet hit him in the back. He went down, rolled. The killer stepped over and shot him again in the chest. Alan stayed still.

A knock sounded on the door of the bed-and-breakfast. She gasped and her heart pounded. The visual of Alan on the floor, shot, bleeding…dead…sent shudders through her even as she stepped to glance through the side window. Lance. She opened the door. "Hi."

"Everything okay?" he asked.

"Yes, why?"

"Toby stopped me and asked me to check on you."

She shook her head and pursed her lips to hide her amusement. "He just walked out the door."

"I know." For a moment, his eyes sparkled with a knowing mirth before turning serious again.

"It's sweet, but honestly. I don't need checking on every two and a half seconds, I promise. As long as you keep anyone from getting in here, I'll be fine. I'm not going anywhere or sneaking out any windows in some dumb attempt to be a hero. I'm going to that lovely library Sabrina has on the second floor, find a good book to sink into and pray I can forget about this mess for a while."

Lance smiled. "That sounds like an excellent plan. You have my number if you need anything though."

"Of course. I really do appreciate it. Thank you, Lance."

"You're very welcome, Robin. I'll probably see you again shortly."

She let out a low chuckle as Lance left with a jaunty salute.

Robin went into the den to sink onto the sofa. For several moments, she stayed put, trying to decide if she wanted to sleep or read.

What she *really* wanted was to remember, but since that didn't present itself as an option, she rose and made her way up the stairs to the library. It was surprisingly well stocked and Robin chose a book she'd loved since childhood.

She returned to the den and for the next hour lost herself in the adventures of a young girl who dreamed of being the first female doctor.

After a short time, she couldn't ignore her rumbling stomach any longer. In the kitchen she fixed a ham and cheese sandwich, all the while keeping an eye on the windows. Knowing Lance and Trent were out there helped keep her nerves at bay, but a restlessness dominated her spirit. She wanted to be helping. Doing something. Pushing the investigation forward.

And the only way she was going to do that was if she remembered. With a sigh, she ate the sandwich, still debating when a shadow passed by the kitchen window. Frowning, she waited, watching to see if it happened again.

It didn't.

She rose and went to the kitchen door. Pushing aside the curtains, she peered out into the backyard. After several seconds of seeing nothing that alarmed her, she blew out a frustrated breath. "You're being paranoid, Robin."

But that didn't mean she didn't have a reason to be. She slipped to the next window. Again nothing.

Robin went to each downstairs window and checked them, making sure they were locked and hadn't been tam-

pered with. None had. But at the front window that over-
looked the main street and the diner, she paused.

Oliver stood talking to Special Agent Young on the
sidewalk. Wait a minute. Wasn't he supposed to be talking
to Toby? Young pulled a piece of paper from his pocket
and flapped it in Oliver's face. Oliver snatched it and
looked at it, then tossed it back at the man.

"What is going on?" she whispered.

Young and Oliver exchanged a few more words, then
Young started her way while Oliver glared after him.

Frowning, she moved to the next window to keep Agent
Young in her sights. Lance stopped him before he got
to the front porch. With a tense jaw and narrowed eyes,
Young began to speak. Robin unlocked the window and
raised it a crack.

"...need to speak with her," Agent Young said. "I have
a request in to a judge to grant us a court order that says
she's to see a Bureau-appointed forensic psychiatrist. But
it would be great if Ms. Hardy would just agree to talk
to him. I promise he'll know how to talk to her, keep her
safe mentally while pulling her memories to the surface."

"No judge would sign such a thing," Lance scoffed.

"We're talking national security. You might be surprised what a judge would sign." When Lance didn't move,
he sighed. "At least ask her if she's willing."

Lance glanced back at the house and blinked when
he saw her watching. She bit her lip. Should she agree
to speak to the psychiatrist? In truth, the thought didn't
bother her, but rather gave her hope. "It's okay, Lance,
let him in."

Agent Young raised a brow and Lance shook his head.
"I don't think so, Robin."

"Please. Just let him in."

Lanced hesitated a moment longer, then shrugged. "Fine, but Toby isn't going to like this."

"Toby's not calling the shots anymore," Young said. "We are."

"We'll see about that," Lance said. He looked at Robin. "Call Toby."

"I will if I need to."

Lance raked a hand over his military-cut hair. "All right then." He eyed the Special Agent. "You won't let her out of your sight, right?"

"I promise."

Lance hesitated another second, then huffed a sigh. "Fine."

"Where's Trent?" Robin called.

"Grabbing us some sandwiches at the diner," Lance said.

"It's open?"

"Part of it. Daisy was determined that the shooter wouldn't make her lose any business."

"Good for her."

"I'll be right here if you need anything, Robin."

"Thanks."

Ignoring Lance's glare, the special agent walked up the steps and Robin met him at the door. "Thank you, Ms. Hardy."

"Robin," she said and gestured to the living area. "We'll be more comfortable in there."

She took a seat on the couch and Special Agent Young took one of the blue wingback chairs next to the fireplace. "Thank you for seeing me," he said again.

"You're welcome, but I thought you and Agent McBride were meeting with Toby."

"McBride is. I decided to let him handle talking to Toby

and come see you. I'm sorry to insist like this, but we really need you to remember that night."

"Waiting until Toby was away to press your advantage was a little sneaky."

He flushed but didn't deny it. "Toby's shared about the virus and we feel like it's supposed to change hands soon. Right now, you're the only person who can stop that from happening."

"I see."

"So, shall we get started?"

She frowned. "I thought I heard you say something about a psychiatrist."

"I did. And that would be me."

"What?"

He clasped his hands between his knees and leaned forward, elbows on his thighs. "Let's talk."

Toby stood from the loveseat and paced to the window. Where was Young? He'd excused himself to get some coffee the minute Toby showed up. McBride sat in the recliner near the window. "How'd you manage to convince the Bureau to pay for the nicest room in the hotel?"

"It was the only one that could serve as an office, too." A pause. "Do you regret leaving the agency?"

Toby turned. "Not really. It was something I felt I had to do. I enjoy teaching and I'm good at it."

"You're good at a lot of things."

"What's that mean?"

"Just that you've managed to keep us from questioning Robin like you know we need to."

"Yeah, well, I have my reasons for that."

"Such as you're in love with her and think we're going to somehow cause her more trauma?"

Toby raised a brow. "Where did that hypothesis come from?"

"Observation. Mostly by my partner. He's really good at reading people."

No kidding. "Robin's important to me," he admitted.

Actually, she was more than just important, but he'd have to address that later when thoughts of loving—and losing—Robin didn't make his knees go weak. "She's remembering more every day," he said. "It's possible she'll remember everything on her own—which is really what the doctor wanted."

"But you don't want her to. Why's that?"

Toby froze. Then met the agent's eyes. Kind eyes. Honest eyes. Toby sighed. "You and I both know the longer she goes without remembering, the more chances a killer has to take her out, so—"

"Exactly. So why won't you let her help us figure this out?"

"It's not that I don't want to help you. Or have Robin help you…" He paused. "I met Robin when she came to work at the university lab shortly after I started teaching there. I really liked her from the first moment I saw her, you know? Unfortunately, I couldn't do anything about it. She was my assignment."

"From Ben."

"Yeah. I had to get close to her—and keep my distance at the same time. It was difficult to say the least."

"I'm sure."

"But you know how it is. The assignment takes precedence over personal feelings."

"You were a good operative."

Toby laughed. "I wasn't an operative at the time, but the training was ingrained. Yeah. I did a good job."

"And still are from what I can tell."

"Thanks." He raked a hand through his hair and glanced down the street one more time. Where was the other agent? A niggling at the back of his mind troubled him, but he couldn't put his finger on the reason. "Your partner coming back any time soon?"

McBride looked at his phone. "He should be back soon I would think."

Toby met the other man's eyes. "He's not getting coffee, is he?"

His phone buzzed and he pulled it from his pocket. A text from Lance. Call me.

FOURTEEN

After telling the agent everything she remembered from the night of the explosion, Robin stood and walked to the mantel and looked at the display of pictures. Family. Friends. People laughing. Making memories. The only memories she had of her parents were angry screams and the blue lights of police cars bouncing on her bedroom walls.

"Robin?"

She drew in a deep breath. "Sorry. Got lost in thought for a moment." She clasped her hands. "But that's all I can tell you. There's nothing more there."

"It's there, you're just going to have to dig a little deeper for it."

But did she want to go digging, that was the question. She decided she must since she'd invited the man into the house to talk to her. "All right. What should I do? How can I pull the memories from this uncooperative brain?"

"We'll go back through the memories with you adding any details that come to mind. So, the trouble started in the lab. You were working."

"Yes. But I have no memory of actually—"

Angry voices caught her attention. She put the slide away and pulled off her gloves.

"Yes," she whispered. "I remember being there." Her excitement grew. "In the lab. I remember! I remembered the men arguing before, but this time I actually remember working before I heard them."

"Who was arguing?"

"Alan and someone. I—I'm not sure. Probably the other man they found dead."

Pop. Pop.

She shuddered. "I'm sorry. I need some water. Would you like some?"

"Sure, I'll take a bottle."

Robin escaped to the kitchen, grabbed a water from the refrigerator and drank half of it. She pulled her phone from her pocket just as it rang. Toby. Just the person she was thinking of calling. "Hello?"

"Robin, I'm glad I caught you. Lance called and said you were talking to Agent Young."

"Yes."

A pause. "All right. I guess if you feel like that's what you need to do, then do it. I don't like the way they went about getting you alone though."

"What do you mean?"

"I have a feeling they pulled me away under the guise of asking me more questions so that Agent Young would have the opportunity to speak to you without me running interference."

"Yes, probably."

"If you have any weird feelings about him, get Lance's attention, please. I'm heading back that way."

"While I don't necessarily like his tactics, I don't get any weird feelings, Toby, I'm fine."

"All right. I'm wrapping up here. See you in a few minutes. And, Robin?"

"Yes?"

"Just…if you remember anything, will you let me know?"

"Of course."

"No matter what it is, you'll tell me?"

"Yes, Toby, I promise. I'll tell you."

"Okay. Thanks."

"Sure. You okay?"

"Yes. We just need to talk."

"Okay. We can do that when you get back. I escaped into the kitchen to get some water and catch my breath, but I think I've kept the man waiting long enough."

"Okay. Take care, Robin."

"Yeah. You, too."

She hung up and a low pop and a loud thud interrupted her. Frowning, she grabbed the bottle of water for the agent, then walked into the den. And gasped. "Agent Young!"

He lay on the floor facedown, a pool of blood gathering beneath his head. She rushed to go to him, then stopped. Her gaze darted around the room. Empty, except for the man who needed help. She started to lift the phone to her ear.

"Put the phone down, Robin," the voice said from behind her. "I've already called it in."

She spun. "Oliver?"

He held his weapon ready while he swept the room.

"What's going on?" she asked, heart pounding, grief welling. "What happened to him?"

"He's been shot."

"By who?" She eyed Oliver's weapon. "You?"

"Of course not. I thought I saw someone slip inside and followed him. We need to get you out of here."

"We need to get him some help."

"And help's on the way. All that matters now is getting

you someplace safe. Now let's go before whoever shot him comes back."

Robin dropped next to the bleeding man on the floor and pressed two fingers to his neck, searching for a pulse. It beat slow and steady. But the bullet hole in his chest didn't bode well.

"Robin, I'm not kidding," Oliver insisted in a low voice. He glanced at the stairs. "We've got to get out of here now."

"We can't just leave him," she said.

"I saw someone sneaking in and came after him. Toby's not here right now, and I've got to keep you safe or he'd never forgive me. I don't know who Young was working with, but they can't be far behind."

"Where are Lance and Trent and the others?"

He hesitated. "I'm not sure. There wasn't anyone watching the house when I walked up."

"That's not possible. I'm calling Toby." She pulled her phone from her pocket and pressed the button to speed dial his number.

Oliver covered her hand with his and squeezed. "Okay, go. Get in my car and lock the doors. Call Toby from there. I'm going to search upstairs," he whispered with another glance at the second floor. "Go."

She hesitated and followed his glance. "No. You come, too. You can't take on a killer all by yourself. You need backup."

He stayed put. Looked at stairs, then back at her. "All right. I'll get you to safety. Come on." He held out a hand, and with one look back at Agent Young, she allowed him to lead her from the room.

Toby hurried out of the motel and climbed into his truck. He'd tried to call Lance twice while McBride had talked about the possibility of a judge signing a court order to mandate that Robin see a psychiatrist to help her bring her memories forward. Toby had nixed that idea and called Lance's number one more time. When he hadn't answered the third time, he'd excused himself and headed for the door.

Before he put the vehicle in gear, he hit Lance's number once more. It rang four times, then went to voice mail. Again. "You said to call you. I'm calling. Pick up."

He tried Robin's phone. Straight to voice mail. He frowned. She had it turned off? That didn't seem right. His worry meter cranked up. Between Lance and Robin not answering, something was wrong. He tried Trent's number.

"Haywood here."

"This is Toby. Have you talked to Lance or Robin lately?"

"No, but he's with Robin. I had to bring food to our drunk-and-disorderly from last night, but I'm planning to head back out to the house to give Lance a break pretty soon."

"Robin decided she was going to speak to Special Agent Young, but I don't have his number. Neither Lance nor Robin are picking up and I'm got a bad feeling. Can you get out there and let me know everything's okay?"

"Of course. I'll leave now and should be there in seconds."

"I'm about five minutes out." Toby hung up and directed the truck to the road. Two minutes away from the house, his phone rang. "Trent?"

"Lance is knocked out cold. Found him in the bushes, pulled out of sight. I've called an ambulance to come get him." Trent paused. "I haven't called Amber yet."

"Robin?"

"No sign of her, Toby, I'm sorry. And Agent Young is

severely wounded on the living room floor. Bullet to his chest."

Toby's heart froze as he pulled behind Trent's vehicle. "I'm here." He let the phone drop from where he had it tucked between his chin and shoulder and shoved it into his pocket. Lance lay on the ground, eyes shut, face pale. But at least he was breathing.

"Clay's on his way here," Trent said. "I used Lance's phone to text him while I was talking to you."

Toby sank to his knees beside the two men. "How bad is it?"

"Pulse is steady, breathing is fine. He's going to have a whopper of a headache, but it's better than a bullet hole."

"How far away is the ambulance?"

The faint sound of the siren answered that for him. Now that Lance was taken care of, Toby's worry for Robin shot up. Where was she? More important, who had her and how was he going to find her?

In the rearview mirror, Robin watched the B&B disappear as Oliver rounded the next corner. "Where are we going?" she asked.

"To a hotel in a neighboring county. You can stay there until Toby can come up with another plan to keep you safe."

He spun the wheel and several folders on the dash slid in front of him. He grabbed them and without taking his eyes from the road, reached back to drop them into the seat behind her.

Her mind blipped. His hands. She'd seen them before. Sweeping files from Alan's workstation.

She gasped.

He slid a glance at her. "What?"

She pressed a hand to her head. "I just had a flash of pain. And I left my medicine at the house."

"I can get you another prescription as soon as we know you're safe."

But she wasn't safe. Not with him.

She glanced at his hands again. Saw them with the files. Holding the weapon that killed Aaron and the other man. Aiming the weapon at her.

"Robin?"

She blinked.

Remembered Toby. Their times together. Everything washed through her mind, flooding it with everything she'd forgotten. Including that horrible, heartbreaking email. Everything flashed in technicolor detail. She closed her eyes and refused to let the memories derail her.

"Yes?"

"Are you okay?"

She forced a smile to her lips. "I'm fine. Just worried."

"About?"

"The fact that someone wants me dead isn't enough?"

"I suppose." He let his eyes linger before snapping them back to the road.

"I'm sorry. My head is starting to pound." She leaned forward, pressing her left hand against her forehead. "Could you find me some pain meds?"

With her right hand, she slid her phone from her pocket and held it next to her right thigh. She tapped the screen with her forefinger. Head down, she glanced at the screen. Nothing. Tapped again. Still nothing.

Instantly, she recalled Oliver covering her hand with his when she'd wanted to call Toby. With that slight pressure and a subtle swipe of his finger, he'd managed to turn the phone off.

She found the power button and pressed it. Hard. Then looked up. "Oliver? Please?"

Narrowed eyes cut her way once more. "I'll stop at the next drugstore we pass."

"Thank you. I'm sorry to be a bother, I'm just worried and scared." She glanced at him, desperate to keep him from realizing she'd turned her phone on.

"You've remembered, haven't you?"

She frowned as though confused. "Yes. Some things. I've already told you that."

"No. You've remembered everything. The lab. The explosion. Me?"

"What would you have done if I'd gotten in the car and called Toby while you searched the house?" she asked.

He slanted a glance at her and she nodded. "You weren't ever going to let me get that far, were you? Telling me to go was just your idea of some kind of reverse psychology. If you were willing to let me walk out of the house and call Toby, I'd have no reason not to trust you."

"You're smart."

He pressed the brake and stopped at the red light. She released her seat belt and swung out hard with her right hand. The phone and her knuckles connected with his cheekbone and she felt the skin split followed by his bellow of pain when his head snapped back to slam against the window. She hit the lock button with her left hand and, still holding her phone in her right, pulled the handle. She tumbled from the sedan and landed hard on her right shoulder.

Horns honked, people screamed.

Fingers wrapped around her left ankle and she turned her back to the asphalt and kicked out with her right foot.

Connected with his nose. Another screech of pain and she was free. She rolled from car, praying she wouldn't get hit by someone else. Robin scrambled to her feet and ran. She had no idea where she was or where she was going, she just knew she had to get away.

"Robin, stop!"

She kept going.

"FBI! Stop that woman!"

But no one reacted other than to watch her run down the sidewalk past the stores and restaurants. She needed a place to hide long enough to call Toby. She glanced at her phone and noted that it was powered up. She lifted it to her mouth and used the voice activation. "Call Toby."

"Calling Toby."

Panting, she rounded a corner and pulled to a stop. Dead end. She bolted back onto the sidewalk and saw Oliver closing the gap. "Please, God, find me a place to hide."

Robin darted into the nearest store. Two customers looked up from the rack of clothes they were perusing. "Where's the nearest police station?" she asked, panting.

"Down the street about a mile on the left," the first woman said, pointing in the direction Robin had just come from. She wasn't going back that way, but maybe she could find a way to loop back around.

Her wide eyes tracked Robin as she made her way to the back of the store. Looping around sounded like the best plan of action. She slipped through the door that led to the rear and found herself in a small office.

The woman at the desk reared back at her entrance. "I'm sorry, this is a private area. You'll have to leave."

"I'm running from a guy who wants to kill me. How do I get out of here?"

The woman pointed to a barely visible door. Boxes and other items were stacked in front of it. "We just got a delivery and then I had to move stuff around while I was looking for something else and I just haven't put them back."

"Help me move them out of the way, please. I can't go back out the front." Had Oliver seen her duck inside?

It was very possible. She lifted the phone to her ear. "Toby?"

No connection. Robin hit Toby's speed dial number once again. It went straight to voice mail. She gave a growl of frustration and tried again. Same thing.

"What's your name?" the woman asked.

"Robin. Yours?"

"Beth."

"Thank you for your help, Beth. Can you call the police, please?"

"Sure." She grabbed the phone and called it in. "They're on the way. Is it an ex?"

"No, I saw someone commit a murder and now he wants to kill me." She paused. "And in case I die before this gets resolved, his name is Oliver Manning and he's an FBI agent."

Beth sucked in a breath and stared. Then hardened her jaw. "Let's get you out of here then."

Together, she and the woman moved the boxes until she saw Beth pause. She stared over Robin's shoulder, eyes wide, mouth open.

Robin tapped Toby's number one more time, then spun to see Oliver holding his gun on them. He wore sunglasses and had pulled on a dark hoodie, but she had no trouble recognizing him. However, he'd be completely anonymous when it came to any security cameras that might capture him running along the sidewalk.

"Drop the phone, Robin," he said. "Now." Without taking his eyes from her, he shifted the weapon to Beth, who was trembling. "Or she dies. You won't have time to turn it on and make a call before I put a bullet in her."

Beth whimpered and Robin dropped the phone onto the desk.

Oliver snagged it and slipped it into his pocket without taking his eyes from hers. "You shouldn't have run." He stepped forward and placed the muzzle against Beth's head. "Let's go or I put one in her head."

Beth gave him a hard shove, and Oliver stumbled backward as she darted for the door. He swung the weapon at Beth, and Robin launched herself at him. She slammed into him even as he pulled the trigger. The bullet burrowed harmlessly into the wall and they both went to the floor.

He recovered faster than she did, gripped her hair in a rough hand and jammed the muzzle against her temple. "You'll pay for that one."

Sirens screamed at the front of the store.

Oliver pulled her, his actions growing frantic.

Resisting would only add to her injuries. She was going to have to bide her time in order to escape. At least Beth had gotten away. "Why didn't you just kill me back there?" she asked.

"I was going to, but decided that wasn't enough."

She frowned and glanced around the alleyway behind the store. Empty. No one even taking out the trash.

"Go, go. They'll be back here fast enough."

"Wasn't enough what?" she asked trying to stall.

"Punishment."

He wasn't going to let her hang back. His grip on her hair moved to her upper arm and he walked fast. She had to almost jog to keep up with his long strides. He pulled her around the side of the building as the first police car appeared at the back of the store.

"Punishment? For me? Because you killed someone, *I* have to be punished for seeing it?"

"Not you. Toby."

FIFTEEN

In frozen disbelief, Toby listened to the conversation. Initially, when he'd heard Oliver's and Robin's voices, relief had flooded him. Until he realized that Oliver was the one behind her kidnapping.

Drop the phone, Robin, he'd said. *Now.* Pause. *Or she dies. You won't have time to turn it on and make a call before I put a bullet in her.*

The words played on a loop through his brain.

Oliver? *Oliver?*

A red blinding rage shuddered through Toby. He clenched his fists and his jaw. *Keep your cool and listen.* He put the phone on mute so no one could hear anything on his side of the line. "Lance, I need to trace this call. Now. Fast."

"...because you killed someone I have to be punished for seeing it?" Robin asked.

"Not you. Toby."

Silence.

"Toby?" Robin finally said. "What does this have to do with him? I saw you kill Aaron and the other man. I saw you steal the files with all of the information about the virus. You're going to sell it."

"Yes, but it was never about the virus. That was simply a moment of opportunity and I took it. It was always about you, Robin. From the moment I saw Toby kiss you on your front porch, retribution was within reach."

Toby's heart stumbled.

"Retri—" A pause. "Retribution for what?"

"Once I realized what Toby was really doing at the university, it was incredibly easy to set him up so I could watch him fall."

"Set him up how? For what?"

Toby couldn't move, couldn't breathe, couldn't think. He could only listen.

The ambulance arrived and Trent grabbed Toby by the arm. "To the station. We can trace the call from there."

"You do realize that Toby's done nothing but lie to you from the beginning," Oliver said.

"Why would you say that?"

"He's an operative for the CIA."

"Ex-operative."

"He told you this time, huh?"

"Yes. And what do you mean 'this time'?"

"So, you haven't remembered the email?"

A pause. "I remember."

Toby flinched and sent up silent prayers as they bolted from the car and into the office at the police station. Trent hooked up the equipment in record time. Once the numbers were entered, the software went to work.

"And you're still going to defend him?" Robin didn't answer. "Before the explosion," Oliver said, "he was making you trust him, convincing you he was a stand-up guy. And you were falling for it. Every last word he said, you believed, and all the while he was just using you to get to the bottom of what was going on at the lab."

"Toby had his reasons for his deceit. And while I was angry and hurt, I really did understand that it was his job.

I was his job." But he'd cared for her, too. He hadn't been able to hide that—or his devastation when she'd told him about the email.

"And you would have forgiven him eventually."

"Yes."

"That's what I figured."

"When did killing me become about Toby? I thought you were his friend."

"We *were* friends. We were tighter than friends. We considered ourselves brothers. And then he led my wife to her death."

"It wasn't his fault," she whispered. "She chose to follow him."

"He told you about that night." Toby registered the shock in Oliver's voice. He grimaced. Oliver knew he never talked about that day. At least not with anyone other than Oliver—or someone he trusted and cared deeply about. Like Robin. And Oliver planned to use that against him.

"Yes," Robin said.

Trent nudged him. "Got it."

"Where?" Toby asked.

"His phone never pinged. Hers did. Looks like he's stopped at a hotel about thirty minutes from here."

"He knows we'd trace his phone so he turned it off," Toby said softly. "But why leave hers on allowing us to do the same exact thing?" He paused. "Is it a trap somehow? You think they're really there?"

"Maybe. If he knows it's connected. He's sure talking like he doesn't have a clue."

"How could he not know? It's got to be a trap."

"We're going to find out," Trent said. "They're still talking, but not moving. I'm going to get some local officers over there ASAP."

"Tell them not to move in. If it's not a trap and he really doesn't know the phone is connected, then we don't want to tip him off without finding out what's going on inside the hotel room." Toby paused. "And let them know what you're driving and wearing. We don't want to get shot by mistake."

"Should we bring in Special Agent McBride here in town?" Trent asked. "He'll have resources we can use."

"I'll call him on the way," Toby said.

"This whole thing is because of what happened to your wife?" Robin asked. "I thought it was about the virus."

"Because that's what I wanted everyone to think. I knew Ben was working on something at the lab, I just hadn't paid attention to what until I realized it was connected to you. Having Alan and Hinkle at the lab that night just made it easier to hide the reason for the explosion. Adding that little piece of evidence behind just reinforced it."

"The paper with the virus structure on it?"

"Yes."

"And thanks to your blips of memory about Alan and Hinkle and their argument, it simply cemented everything. That was incredibly helpful in throwing the investigation off. What better way to get away with something when the people investigating believe something that isn't true?"

"So, if I had died in the blast, then you would have just sold the virus, taken the money and retired to some beach community?"

"Nope, I still would have kept working. You can't spend that kind of money immediately, you know."

Robin shuddered.

"And besides, I would have wanted to hang around to see the aftermath of your death. Watch my *friend* grieve the loss of the woman he loved." Oliver's eyes narrowed and he drew in a deep breath. "However, since that's not how this is going to play out thanks to the incompetent fools I hired and your unwillingness to die, I've had to revamp the plan."

He was awful. A man so blinded, scarred by bitterness and hate that he couldn't see past the deception—that his wife had made the choice that led to her death. It wasn't Toby's fault. Only Oliver couldn't see it. "Oliver, Toby doesn't love me. Not like you loved your wife. So, this whole revenge plot is for nothing. Yes, he'll care that I die, but it won't damage him for life. He'll get over it and move on. He'll find someone else."

"You're wrong." He waved the weapon at her. "Get out."

Oliver had pulled into the parking lot of a motel and stopped in front of room 105. "What are you doing?" Robin asked.

"You're going to call Toby and tell him he's going to meet us."

"Where?"

"At the location I'm going to give you. I think I can get this plan back on track."

"Why? You just said you wanted to kill me and then hang around and watch him suffer. How is calling him out here going to help you do that?"

"And I just told you that I had to revamp the plan. Getting Toby and you together is all that matters right now. He's going to watch you die just like I watched my wife die."

"And then you'll kill Toby, right?" she asked.

He shrugged.

"He'll bring backup," she said. "You know that."

"Not if he cares about you."

He was too far gone to reason with. She blinked. "So,

how are you going to get away to enjoy all your lovely money you're going to get from the sale of the virus? Toby will come with the intent to stop you." She prayed the phone was still connected and Toby was somehow tracing it, but couldn't count on that. She walked toward the motel room, heart thundering. Should she cooperate? Fight back? *God, please tell me what to do!*

"Shut up and open the door." Oliver passed her the key and she swiped it across the door with a desperate glance over her shoulder.

"No one's coming. Get in there." He gave her a rough shove and she stumbled inside.

It wasn't the dump she'd expected. Instead of the regular two-bed motel room, she found herself standing in a living area. A small kitchen dominated the left corner and she figured the door to her right led to the bedroom and bath. "What now?"

He pulled out her phone and passed it to her. "Call him."

She took the phone and tapped the screen. Hope leaped. Still connected.

Oliver snatched it from her. Stared at it for a split second, gave a scream of rage and threw it across the room.

Toby blinked. "What was that?"

"Sounded like something hit the floor," Trent said.

"Did we lose the signal?"

"No. It's still there."

A door slammed. Then silence.

Toby pressed fingertips to the bridge of his nose. "He figured out the line was connected."

"Yeah, sounds like. He didn't bother to turn off the phone because he doesn't plan to be there by the time we arrive."

"How far away are we from the motel?" Toby asked.

"Five minutes. Local cops should have the place surrounded."

"Tell them not to confront him. If he's provoked, there's no telling what he'll do, but tell them to follow him."

The miles passed as quickly as if they were slogging through quicksand and all Toby could do was pray.

Trent's radio crackled to life. He'd connected to the local police channel. "Suspect and his hostage are in the wind. Repeat. We've lost them."

Toby's heart dropped. "No," he whispered. But wasn't surprised. Oliver knew all of the ins and outs of losing a tail. He wasn't going to be as easy to apprehend as a run of the mill criminal.

Finally Trent turned into the parking lot of the motel and Toby loosened the fists he hadn't realized he'd made.

Special Agent McBride pulled alongside them and stepped out. Walked over. "They lost them. Let me know what you need, and I can make it happen."

"We need to check the security footage." Toby pointed. "There's a camera there and there. If they're on this side of the building, I'm willing to believe they're on the other side."

"If they're working," Trent muttered.

"This isn't a run-down place. It's well maintained and has a good reputation around here." Toby narrowed his eyes. "If Oliver had a room here, I want to see it." He ran a hand over his chin and realized he was shaking. "He was in a hurry. We disrupted whatever his plan for Robin and this place was. He's having to think on his feet which means there's a higher possibility he'll mess up. We need to keep the pressure on."

"I'm with you," Trent said. "Let's get that footage."

Toby led the way to the office while his heart continued to pound a frantic rhythm, urging him to hurry, reminding him Robin was in danger and it was his fault. Like he needed the reminder.

Inside the office, Trent flashed his badge at the young woman behind the counter. Her name badge read Karen S. "Hi, Karen, we need your help."

Her eyes widened. "Sure. What can I do for you?"

"Do your security cameras work?"

"Of course."

"Great." He told her what they needed and the time frame to search. Karen led them to a back room where she pulled up the footage.

Toby watched, hating the minutes that were now flying past too fast. "There," he said, pointing at the screen. "Back it up a bit and pause."

She did so.

"There they come. Out of room 105," Trent said.

"He took her, didn't he?" Karen asked.

"Yes. There. You can see the weapon in her lower back." Just saying the words sent his heart pounding even harder. Oliver and Robin disappeared from the camera for a few heart-stopping moments. Then reappeared when they hurried across the parking lot.

"The old sedan is his," Karen said. "I was here when he checked in earlier today."

The sedan backed out of the parking spot and headed for the exit. Then turned left. The police cruiser followed shortly thereafter.

And no doubt Oliver noticed.

"He may try to switch cars at some point." He turned to Agent McBride, who'd followed them inside but had up to this point stayed quiet. "Can you run the plate?" Toby asked.

McBride pulled out his phone. "Give it to me."

Toby did and continued watching the footage, only there was nothing else to see.

McBride cleared his throat. "The sedan was reported stolen this morning around seven o'clock from an apartment complex not too far from here."

"Stolen. Of course it was. And he's probably on his way to steal another."

"I'll put out a BOLO on the sedan and a description of each of them," McBride said. "Let's check the room and see if he left any indication where he may be headed."

Trent looked at Toby. "This guy was your friend. Any idea?"

"No." Toby held out his hand to Karen. "Key, please?"

She slapped a plastic card into his palm. "It's a master. It opens all the doors."

"Thanks."

They hurried out of the motel office and down the side of the building to room 105. Officers blocked off the area around the room, and even though Toby and Trent had seen Oliver and Robin leave, they still approached with caution. Toby stopped at the edge of the door. Trent took the other side and Agent McBride nodded his readiness, as well.

Toby swiped the card and shoved the door open. Trent rounded the doorjamb followed by Agent McBride. Toby brought up the rear.

"Clear!" Trent called from the bedroom.

Toby and McBride covered the rest of the small area and cleared it quickly. Trent joined them in the living area.

In the kitchen, Toby spotted something wedged under the refrigerator. "Need a glove," he said.

Trent passed him one and Toby used it to slide the object out from under the fridge. "It's Robin's phone." He stood. "Let's see what else we can find in here."

It didn't take long to turn up nothing except a suitcase with several changes of clothing. "The motel clerk said Oliver just checked in this morning," Trent said. "I'm guessing anything of importance, he kept on him. Or in his vehicle."

"Yeah." Toby swiped a hand across his eyes. "Any word on the BOLO?"

"Not yet."

Now how were they going to find Robin?

SIXTEEN

Robin glanced at Oliver from the corner of her eye and debated opening the door and rolling out once again. This time, however, her hands were cuffed in front of her. Only the fact that they were on the highway and he didn't seem inclined to slow down kept her from pulling the door handle just like she'd done before.

Stuffing her fear deep down, she drew in a slow breath. Trying to calm her racing pulse was a futile effort. "Where are we going?"

"Someplace where I can take a minute to think and figure things out."

A muscle jumped in his tight jaw and she had a feeling he was slightly panicked at the turn things had taken, but was able to think on his feet thanks to his profession. "The other guy you killed at the lab. Who was he?"

"A guy by the name of Reese Hinkle. I'd seen him around and talking to Alan quite a bit while I was watching you. I thought it odd those two were talking, but didn't really care what they were up to. You were my focus."

"And the other two men? Holloway and Olander?"

"Holloway blew up a convenience store and killed two people. I tracked him down about a year ago and decided to let him go as long as he kept his nose clean."

"A killer?"

"A killer with a skill I thought I might be able to use one day."

She swallowed. "You were already planning your revenge at that point, weren't you?"

"Not in detail, but…" He shrugged.

Robin shuddered. She didn't want to hear any more about that. "I remember the email," she said.

He gave a short nod. "It was only a matter of time."

"What were you hoping I'd do after I read it?"

"Exactly what you did. You pushed him away, he was hurt, and he was furious with the person who sent it—me."

"So…"

"So…" He clicked his tongue and shook his head. "Toby came to see me, told me what was going on and asked me to look into the email. He also said he was going to do everything in his power to earn your forgiveness and trust back. You should have seen him. He was so torn up. I'd never seen Toby beat himself up over anything like that before. Except Debra's death."

"And you couldn't bring yourself to forgive him—even though her death wasn't his fault."

"Yes, it was! It was his fault and now your death is going to be his fault, too!"

"No, Oliver, if I die that's on your hands."

"Shut up! Don't say another word."

Robin closed her eyes. The hurt and sheer betrayal she'd felt when she'd read that email washed over her in a fresh wave. But with it came a sense of determination. Toby hadn't wanted to deceive her. He'd simply been doing his job when he'd met her. It was only later, after getting to know her, that he'd hated the necessary deception and wanted to make it right. He'd told her exactly that when she confronted him about the email. He'd been shocked.

Literally dizzy with the knowledge that someone would betray him like that. He'd immediately apologized, but at the time she hadn't wanted to hear it.

However, Oliver's words broke her heart. And after being with Toby over the last few days, seeing him in action, she now had a better understanding of why he had acted as he had.

Unfortunately, Toby had been stuck between a rock and a hard place and he'd gone to the man he'd considered a friend and poured his heart out. He'd expressed his remorse over lying to her and wanted to make it right. And Oliver had betrayed him in a most deadly way.

Now, she just wanted to hug Toby. And have the chance to kiss him again without any regrets between them. "I want to talk to Toby."

"No."

"Why not?"

"Because not knowing where you are is killing him. I'll just let him suffer a little longer." He paused. "He tracked us to the motel via your phone. Now he doesn't have that lifeline to cling to. The hope that he'll get to you in time. Now he's scrambling and it's making him crazy."

"Well, talking to him isn't going to change that. You're going to kill me in the end—someone who had absolutely nothing to do with your wife's death. I'm completely innocent, and I have just one request before I die and that's to talk to Toby. I think you owe me that at least." The words slipped out before she could think to filter them. She bit her lip, worried she'd gone too far.

His jaw tightened and he flexed his fingers around the wheel. "Fine. I'll find a place to pull over. But if this is an effort to give him another phone to trace, it won't work. It's not possible to track this one. Just like the pitiful attempts to follow us from the hotel didn't work." Disgust curled his lip. "He thinks I'm an amateur. He really should know better."

About two minutes later, he pulled into an empty church parking lot and parked in the middle of it. No cars around them meant no help. A closed church building meant no unlocked door to escape into. Traffic was far enough away that trying to flag someone down would be impossible. Oliver had chosen well.

She held her hand out and he placed the phone into it.

"No video, just voice," he said.

She dialed Toby's number. He picked up before the ring had finished. "What?"

"Toby?"

"Robin! Are you okay? Where are you?"

Oliver scowled and reached as though to grab the phone from her. She dodged his grasping fingers. If he was going to take the phone, she was going to make him work for it. "I don't know where I am," she told Toby. It was the truth. She could give him the exit number off the interstate, but that was it. She'd never seen a sign for the name of a town. Oliver backed down when she didn't try to say something he didn't like. "He let me call you to tell you goodbye." Just saying the words brought a lump to her throat, but she wasn't wasting time crying through this phone call.

"Why?"

"I don't know that either, but I just wanted you to know that I appreciate everything you did to protect me and that whatever happens, none of this is your fault. I forgive you, so—"

Oliver yanked the phone from her and placed it to his ear. "It is your fault. All of it."

He hung up and Robin wanted to scream out her fear and frustration at the interruption. She hadn't said nearly all that she wanted to. Instead she swallowed hard and clenched her teeth while her brain scrambled for a plan. But as long as she didn't know their destination, it was hard to come up with something.

"They'll be looking for this car, you know."

"I know."

He didn't sound too worried about it. Oliver pulled out of the church parking lot and drove another ten minutes before turning into a motel parking lot that looked very similar to the one they'd just run from. "Sit tight. Don't move. Don't even think about it. If you bring attention to yourself, I'll just have to kill whoever responds, understand?"

She understood. The look in his eyes said he wasn't kidding. He'd do whatever it took to accomplish his end goal and hurt whomever he had to hurt.

Robin stayed put but quickly analyzed the area. Two people climbed into a van. A mother stood at the door to her room with a toddler on her hip. She opened the door and slipped inside. The room next to her stood open, a housekeeping cart blocking the entrance.

"Okay," he said.

"Okay what?"

He cranked the SUV and pulled up to the covered entrance to the motel office and parked just outside the automatic sliding glass doors. He'd chosen a motel again instead of a hotel. No inside rooms for Oliver. He wouldn't want to be trapped inside should something go wrong. Robin was scrambling to make things go wrong anyway.

He handcuffed her to the SUV's door handle. "I'll be watching. Right now, you decide who lives or dies. You get anyone's attention and they're dead, you got it?"

She bit her lip.

He grabbed her chin and jerked her around to look at him. "I said, got it?"

His fingers bit into her skin. "Yes. Got it." She wished

she dared to actually spit in his face, but figured it would be better to remain calm and not provoke him.

He released her and she raised her free hand to touch her face. The cuts from the window glass had scabbed over, but she still felt like she looked rough. Could she use that to her advantage?

A patrol car pulled into the parking lot and she sat up straighter, shooting a look into the lobby of the motel. Oliver had his profile to her. A quick turn of his head and he could easily see her.

The officer parked and climbed out of his vehicle. Robin watched him approach. His eyes never stilled as they probed back and forth. He was an officer like so many. Men and women who never truly felt safe when they were wearing the uniform and who stayed alert for any threat. To them or someone else.

As he crossed in front of her, his gaze snagged hers. She locked her eyes on him and followed his progress to the front of Oliver's car. He paused. She stared. He started toward her when Oliver opened the driver's door.

The officer nodded to Oliver and continued into the motel. Robin closed her eyes and let out a slow breath.

Oliver slid into the driver's seat. "You're not trying any funny business, are you? I don't mind killing cops."

"I get it, Oliver," she snapped. "I'm not doing anything."

"But you're thinking about it."

"Well, thinking and doing are two completely different things, aren't they?"

He shot her a hard look and drove them around to the side of the building where he'd initially stopped. The housekeeping cart was now at the next room with the young woman dressed in black slacks and a blue shirt rummaging for rolls of toilet paper underneath.

"You killed Ben, didn't you?" Robin asked.

"Ben figured out something he shouldn't have."

"What was that?"

"That the only way you and Toby could have been traced to Wrangler's Corner was through me. He called me on it."

"So, you killed him and set it up to look like an accident."

"I did."

When the cleaning woman disappeared back into the room, Oliver got out of the SUV and rounded it to open the passenger door. He uncuffed her from the handle but kept the second cuff on her wrist. "Let's go."

He led her to the room, opened the door and shoved her inside.

Toby slammed a fist on the dash of the vehicle and Trent shot him a sideways glance. "Are you going to be all right?"

"That remains to be seen. Robin's still in the hands of a lunatic. One of my best friends." Toby scoffed. "I can't believe I didn't see this. How could he have fooled me like this for so long?"

"From what you've said, you were both working. You weren't really around him that much, were you?"

"No. Not much, but we talked occasionally."

"Who called first when you talked?"

Toby hesitated, then rubbed his eyes. "I did." He thought about all the times he'd called and Oliver hadn't picked up—or called him back. "But I didn't think anything about it. He was my grieving friend and I was calling to check on him. I mean, I knew he was having a hard time and I even recommended he talk to a counselor, but this…" He shook his head. "I never would have suspected this. Every time I brought it up, he said he didn't blame me, that he should have seen it, that it was his fault. Not once did he let on that he blamed me." Toby blew out a low breath. "All this time, he's blamed me and his bitterness just kept growing while he plotted his revenge. Unbelievable. I can't even wrap my brain around it."

"Grief can do strange things to people."

"Yeah. No kidding."

Trent's phone rang. He put it on the vehicle's Bluetooth. "Agent McBride, what do you have?"

"I got a call from one of the agents investigating the bombing of the lab. They've identified the other man and are now searching his apartment."

"Good," Toby said.

"Another thing, a call came in a few minutes ago from an officer along Interstate 40. He spotted the BOLO vehicle and started to tail it, then it disappeared."

"He lost it?"

"Yeah."

"Where's the last place he saw it?"

"Exit 65."

"So that's where we need to head," Toby said.

"Manning could have spotted the tail, got off on the exit, hid somewhere and then got back on the interstate."

"Maybe," Toby said, "and maybe Oliver wasn't even in that vehicle. He could have traded it out and gotten someone else to drive it down the highway to throw us off, but it's a start." He shot a desperate glance at the deputy. "We've got nothing else. We have to run with what we've got."

Trent nodded and aimed the car toward the interstate with Agent McBride still on the line. "We're flying blind here, Toby, you know that, right? This is a major long shot."

"I know. But I also know Oliver. He's a thinker and a

planner. If he stays true to his personality, he'll want to find a place to hole up and think. To plan."

"Another motel?"

"Probably. And he's going to want to unload that virus."

"Agent McBride," Toby said, "has there been any chatter about some kind of auction? Anyone selling a virus to the highest bidder?"

"No. Nothing. If they're talking about it, they're doing it offline, but we're checking other resources to see if they've heard anything."

"Great. Let me know if you hear anything else?"

"Of course."

Toby sent up prayers as Trent sped up and they headed for the exit where he could only pray they'd find Robin alive.

Seated on the floor and cuffed to the leg of the bed while Oliver paced from one end of the room to the other, Robin had managed to come up with a sort-of-but-not-really plan. The question was could she make it work. Then again, what choice did she have? If she failed, she could die. If didn't try, she *would* die.

"I need to use the restroom."

He stopped his pacing and held up his phone. "I have a plan." His eyes narrowed and he brought his weapon up to aim it at her.

She flinched. He laughed. A shudder swept through her and the fear that she'd managed to keep under control up to this point came close to consuming her. "What's your plan, Oliver?" she asked softly.

"To FaceTime with Toby. He'll watch every minute. Of course I won't be on camera. Can't be stupid about this."

"Oliver...please!"

"Don't worry, I'll be sure to let you say hello first."

"Everyone knows it was you, Oliver. Why continue this? There's no way you'll ever be a free man again."

"Maybe not in this country, but there are other places to live."

Panic squeezed her lungs. Pain thudded at the back of her head. "Oliver? Can I please use the bathroom?"

He blinked. "Why?"

"Why? Because I'm human! I'm a person and I need to use the bathroom!" She bit her lip, grappling with her tears and terror. *God, please, be merciful and let it be fast if I'm to die, but I really don't want to die yet. I've got too much to live for.*

Oliver stepped up beside her and released the cuffs. "Fine. But no funny business or you'll hurt for a long time, understand?"

"Yes." She slipped into the bathroom and stuffed her fist against her mouth to keep her sobs and screams at bay. He was going to FaceTime with Toby and kill her while Toby watched. Then he'd leave the motel, get in his car and find a way to sell the virus to the highest bidder. Then live off the grid for the rest of his days. If he could make it work. He certainly had the skills to make it a real possibility.

Robin stared at the toilet tank lid. It had worked before. Could she dare hope it would work again? Only one way to find out. She hefted it from its resting place and held on to the bottom.

And waited.

It didn't take long. A hard fist pounded on the door. "Time's up!"

She stayed quiet.

More pounding. "Robin! Don't make me come in there!"

Robin bit her lip and refused to let her tears fall or the terror distract her. This was it.

Something slammed against the door and it shuddered in the frame. A squeak left her lips, but she doubted he heard it as he used either his foot or his shoulder to crash against the door again and again.

It was a lot more sturdy than she thought it would be.

"Robin! I'm going to kill you!"

Another loud bang against the door and it flew inward. Robin swung the lid with everything in her, slamming it into his midsection. He cried out and went to the floor. Robin rushed past him. A hard hand caught her knee. She kicked out, swung a fist and connected. And she was free. Not stopping, she rushed from the bathroom and yanked open the outside room door with a frantic glance over her left shoulder.

Oliver stood in the doorway of the bathroom, weaving. Blood ran from a gash on his forehead. He stepped forward, then stumbled to his knees. He lifted the weapon he still held in his right hand.

Cold air blasted Robin as she bolted from the room and turned left on the sidewalk.

Panic gripped her. She hadn't knocked him out cold like she'd hoped she would. That meant she had very little time. His angry roar reached her as Robin ran faster, aiming for the only hiding place she could think of.

A shot rang out and Robin screamed when a burning pain hit her in the back.

SEVENTEEN

Toby held on as Trent swung the squad car into the parking lot of the motel. The officer who'd called in to report Oliver and Robin's location waved them to a stop. Toby leaped out of the vehicle. "Where is she?"

"They're in room 112. This way."

A low scream reached them and they took off toward it with Toby leading the way. He rounded the corner and pulled to a stop. Oliver stumbled along the sidewalk. "Oliver!"

The agent turned. Surprise pulled his brows up, then fury lit his eyes. He dashed down the sidewalk.

"Oliver! Stop!"

"I'm not going to prison!"

"Where's Robin?" Toby hurried after his former friend. Trent and an officer named Wilkes followed, weapons ready.

Oliver darted into the stairwell, lifted his weapon and fired.

Toby ducked behind the nearest car and knew Trent and Wilkes had done the same. "It's over, Oliver. You know how this is going to end if you don't stop it now."

Helicopter blades beat the air above. More police cars squealed into the lot.

"I'm not ready to give up yet, Tobe, sorry."

"Where's Robin?"

"She's dead."

Toby's heart stopped for a brief moment and he swallowed hard. "I'll believe that when I see her."

"How's it feel, Toby? To know you're helpless? That you couldn't do anything to save her?"

Dear God, please let him be lying.

Officers continued to spread out and surround the building. "Oliver, give it up. You don't have to die today."

Oliver gave a harsh laugh. "I died the day you killed my wife."

"Maybe you should take responsibility for that one. You never said a word about her being so distraught over you and your job or that you were having issues. How was I supposed to know what was going on? You were her husband. I was your friend. And you never say anything? No way, Oliver. Her death isn't because of me. It's because of you!"

"How dare you?" Oliver hovered at the corner, trapped near the vending machines, protected by the small area. He waved his weapon. "Tell them to clear out. This is between you and me, Toby."

"Put the weapon down now!" The voices of various law enforcement rang out, one after the other, with the order.

"No, it's not," Toby said. "It's over. Now, where's Robin?"

"I told you. She's dead. You're too late! I shot her!"

His heart dropped. The man almost had him convinced. "Then at least tell me where she is so I can say goodbye."

Movement in the doorway of the room next to Oliver captured his attention. The housekeeping cart shifted, started to roll. A woman darted from the open doorway right in front of Oliver.

Quicker than Toby could blink, the agent snagged

her by the hair and pulled her against him, jamming his weapon against her temple. "Now back off!" Oliver yelled as he moved away from the vending room. The woman screeched over Oliver's order.

Shouts and commands echoed around him. Toby calculated whether he could make the shot. He thought he could, but at what cost? Would Oliver pull the trigger with the impact of Toby's bullet?

"All of you, back off!" Oliver shifted the weapon and pointed it for one brief second at Toby.

A figure shot out from behind the housekeeping cart and slammed into Oliver's back. He gave a harsh grunt and stumbled, releasing his hold on his hostage but keeping his grip on his weapon. The housekeeper bolted.

Robin! She grappled with Oliver, who swung his weapon to her head.

Toby fired. Three shots center mass.

Oliver stilled. His weapon dropped. He staggered backward and went to his knees. Agent McBride, Toby and Trent raced toward the wounded man.

Toby grabbed Robin up against him. "Are you okay?" His right hand landed in a warm wetness on her back. "You're hurt!"

"It's okay. He shot at me when I ran, but it's just a graze, I think."

Two ambulances turned in to the parking lot. "Great timing," Toby said. "Let's get you looked at."

He turned toward the first ambulance, his gaze landing on Oliver Manning, who lay still on the ground. Agent McBride and Trent knelt next to him. "He had a vest on," Trent said. "He's going to hurt for a while, might even have a couple of cracked or broken ribs, but he'll live."

Gratitude crashed over Toby. He hadn't wanted to see

the man dead, but when Oliver had turned his weapon on Robin, Toby'd had no choice. "Thanks."

The paramedic and Toby helped Robin into the back of the ambulance. The woman examined the area and jutted her chin at Toby. "Are you her husband?"

"No, I'm—"

"Then get out for a minute, please." Her eyes softened. "I'll let you know when you can come back in."

Loathe to leave Robin now that he'd just managed to get her safe, he hesitated.

"It's okay, Toby," Robin said. "Go check on Oliver."

He didn't want to check on Oliver, he wanted to stay with Robin, but with a sigh, he backed up and gave Robin her privacy.

A hand settled on his shoulder and he turned to find Clay there. "Hey, how is she?" the deputy asked.

"Alive. That's all that matters to me."

"She was hurt?"

"Some fragment from where the bullet struck the wall." Toby drew in a deep breath. The first one he'd taken since learning of Robin's kidnapping. "But she's going to be all right." He paused. "How's Oliver?"

"Paramedics have him in the other ambulance. Go see him."

Oliver was the last person Toby wanted to see, but he needed to. He found him sitting in the back of the ambulance just as Clay had said. Under heavy guard, his former friend looked worn and beaten. Oliver's gaze met his and the empty expression in the man's eyes chilled Toby. "Things could have been so different, man."

Oliver pursed his lips and breathed in. Then winced. "I don't think so. Once I got past the shock of losing Debra, I needed someone to blame. You were it."

"You never let on."

"Because I hated myself for blaming you. Then it just became second nature. Then I wanted to hurt you as much as I was hurting."

Toby nodded and looked away for a moment. "I'm going to miss the man I thought you were," he finally said. "I hope I can forgive you one day."

Oliver's gaze slid from his. "I don't want or need your forgiveness. Just go away, Toby."

"Maybe you don't, but I do." A grief tinged with anger invaded Toby's emotions. A grief that was similar to losing a loved one. Which he'd done. Oliver, his friend, was as dead as if he was buried six feet under.

Toby left and made his way back to Robin's ambulance. She stood just outside the doors, wearing a scrubs top in place of her bloody T-shirt. He wrapped his arms around her and pulled her close. "You scared me," he whispered.

She gave him a gentle shove and he stepped back. "I remembered the email," she said.

Toby's face dropped and he shoved his hands into the front pockets of his jeans. "I'm sorry, Robin," he said. "I wanted to tell you, but—"

She placed a finger over his lips. "Shh."

His lips snapped together.

"I remembered the email, and I'm not mad about it anymore. I think it's time to move past that."

He grabbed her and hugged her, squeezing the breath from her.

"Toby? I need to breathe."

And then she was free. Or rather, his hold loosened. "Can I tell you something?" he asked.

"Of course." Wetness dropped on her cheeks and she gasped. "It's snowing!"

"I ordered that for you," he said. With a look over his

shoulder, he gripped her hand and pulled her away from the chaos to load her in a Wrangler's Corner deputy's cruiser. He climbed in beside her. "Okay, so here's the deal. I used to love my job with the CIA. I got to go to some really cool places and do some really cool things. I also had to deal with the dregs of humanity."

"I'm sorry."

He shrugged. "It was what I chose to do, and I was good at it. While home, here in the states, I taught."

"I know. International studies and cultures."

"You do remember."

She nodded. "Everything."

"When Ben got a tip something weird was going on at the university lab, he knew I was there full-time. He also knew I didn't want to get back into the whole espionage game, but he convinced me he needed me. That everyone in the lab was in potential danger."

"From what? The virus?"

Toby grimaced. "Ben never said that was what was going on exactly, but I think he suspected it. Alan Roberts and the other man who was killed had been meeting in secret for several months. The only problem was we couldn't catch them doing anything suspect. We couldn't even get a listening device close enough to hear what they discussed at their meetings. Which were always held in public places with lots of noise. But the night they died, the feds picked up something about an auction and delivery. They were able to track down several of the bidders who are now being rounded up in various countries."

"But Oliver said he didn't know anything about the virus or the lab. He was simply there to kill me to get revenge on you and saw stealing the virus and planting the paper as a way to throw the investigation of the bombing off—and make a lot of money as a bonus if he could sell the virus."

"Not every agent knows every case other agents are working on," Toby said, "so it doesn't surprise me that Oliver was clueless." He shrugged. "He wasn't really doing his job anyway from what's getting back to me. He'd been reprimanded several times over the last few months for various infractions."

"He was too focused on plotting his revenge."

"Exactly."

She rubbed her eyes and shook her head. "I can't believe Alan was capable of anything underhanded like that," Robin said. "He always seemed so jovial and upbeat—even with his daughter's leukemia diagnosis. He's the last person I would suspect of being willing to betray his country. Because that's what it amounts to."

"I agree."

"Oliver wasn't in on the virus thing. He just happened to be there planning to kill me when he overheard the conversation between Alan and Hinkle. He decided at the last minute to take advantage of the opportunity and steal the virus—with the intention of selling it to the highest bidder."

"He told you that?"

"Yes."

He sighed and rubbed his eyes. "Robin, it was never my intent to hurt you like I did. Ben caught the case and asked for my help. I arranged to meet you and I'll admit, it was my goal to gain your trust."

"Which you did. Very easily."

"Yes." He cleared his throat. "Which let me know almost immediately that if something was going on at the lab, you weren't involved in it."

"Well, thank you for that." She paused. "It was the dimples."

He blinked. "What?"

"They come across as very trustworthy."

"My dimples?"

"Well, not them specifically." She gave a low laugh. "But they make you appear boyish and innocent. Trustworthy."

"Oh."

"That's probably why you were so good at your covert operations."

"Maybe, but that's not important anymore. You're important. I hope you understand that I really wanted to tell you when you asked me what we'd argued about. I was just so afraid if I told you—or if you remembered—you'd demand I leave you alone and I would be forced to go."

"I probably would have," she said. "I was pretty mad."

"If that was pretty mad, I really don't want to see you furious. And…" he breathed deep "…you were wrong."

"About what?" She lifted a brow.

"About when you told Oliver that I don't love you."

Robin's throat tightened and she blinked against the annoyingly insistent tears. She didn't want to miss this moment because she couldn't see through a blur of liquid. "What are you saying, Toby?"

"I'm saying that I do love you. I've loved you for a long time. I just couldn't admit it because I didn't want to tell you with all the lies between us—which I take full responsibility for. I just hope you can forgive me one day."

Heart hammering in her throat, Robin reached out to pull him close. "Like I told you when I was in the car with Oliver and thought we were having our last conversation, I forgive you."

She pressed her lips to his. To her relief, Toby didn't

hesitate. He gathered her closer and she let herself melt against him.

"What are you doing for Christmas?" he asked against her mouth.

"Um…what I usually do…nothing. Why?"

He reared back. "Nothing? Nothing? You can't do nothing on Christmas!"

She dug a finger in her ear. "You're shouting."

"Because I'm appalled."

"Well, I'm sorry. I've never had a 'real' family for Christmas. You know how it was in foster care. You might be in the room for Christmas, but you knew you didn't belong."

He tilted her chin. "I know. I remember those days before I reconnected with Zoe and Aaron and they welcomed me in, making me a part of their family without hesitation. But for you? Never again, okay?"

She nodded and was going to have try to see through the tears after all. "So." She cleared her throat. "What are you doing for Christmas?"

"Spending it—and I hope every one thereafter—with you."

"I love you, Toby," she whispered.

"I love you, too, Robin."

Excitement swirled within her. She wasn't sure what she'd done to deserve this amazing man, but she sent up a prayer of thanks for the blessing God had dropped into her life. As he held her, then kissed her and as the snow fell around them, Robin knew she'd finally come home.

Christmas Day
Three weeks later

Robin stood in the midst of chaos and found herself loving every minute of it. *This* was the Christmas she'd

dreamed of all her life. Her throat tightened, but she refused to cry. There was too much to take in to have to try
to see it all through a blur of tears.

The entire Starke clan had gathered at Aaron and Zoe's
home. While large, the ranch-style house seemed like it
might burst at the seams any moment now. Snow covered
the ground and more kept falling. They were going to get
snowed in and no one seemed to care one bit.

A squeal reached her seconds before her leg was taken
hostage by a pint-size hurricane. "*Hep* me, Birdie."

Birdie. Grace's nickname for Robin. When they'd been
introduced, she'd giggled. "Robins are birds. You a birdie!"

"Sophia loves birds," Toby had explained. "Apparently,
she's passed down some knowledge to her little sister."

Robin grabbed the child up in her arms just as Sophia
barreled into the room with narrowed eyes.

"Grace, why is Sophia chasing you?"

"Game!" Grace shook a small box she held in her right
hand.

Sophia stomped over, mouth pursed, but laughter in
her gaze. "She took Uncle Toby's present."

"Now, Grace, you better give that back to Toby," Robin
said with a smile. She looked over Sophia's shoulder to
see Toby watching them with a sappy look on his face.
Her heart flipped like it always did when she found him
looking at her with love in his eyes. So much love it was
almost like he had a hard time containing it.

"What's in the box?" Robin asked.

"Ring," Grace said.

Robin blinked. Toby walked slowly toward her, wad-
ing through the sea of larger boxes and wrapping paper.
Her vision narrowed. "A ring?"

Grace nodded and grinned wider. Even Sophia was

practically dancing out of her shoes. Robin met Toby's gaze. "What's this all about?"

"I was going to wait until a little later to do this, but it seems my plans have been altered—which can happen when you have a super smart two-year-old who likes to pick your pockets hanging around." He held his hand out to Grace. "May I please have the box, you little thief?"

"No." She shook her head. "Mine."

"Oh, Gracie…" Sophia singsonged from behind Toby. "Guess what I have?" Grace's gaze latched onto the stuffed animal her sister held. "You want to hold him?"

"Down, Birdie," Grace demanded.

"Please," Toby reminded.

"Pwease," Grace echoed.

Robin set the child on the floor while Toby snatched the box from her little hand. Grace didn't seem to notice, her goal the little bunny in her sister's hand.

"Sophia will watch her for a bit. You want to grab our coats and step outside with me?"

Robin bit her lip and her stomach turned flips. Knowing eyes followed them out the door, but no one stopped them or even attempted to talk to them.

Toby led her out in to the falling snow and down to the dock where he pulled her close and nuzzled her neck. "I've loved spending these last three weeks with you. All of our time together has simply cemented what I've known for a while now."

"What's that?"

"You're the one I want to spend the rest of my life with, Robin. Please tell me you feel the same."

She smiled. "You know I do."

He huffed a short laugh and his breath frosted in the air. "Well, yeah, I kind of figured, but hearing you say it is nice." He kissed her once. Twice. Then lifted his head and locked his gaze on hers. "You're an amazing woman, Robin Hardy. Will you marry me?"

The lump in her throat prevented any words from escaping. All she could do was sniff. And nod. Vigorously.

Toby laughed, kissed her again and opened the box. "It was my grandmother's. Even being bounced from foster home to foster home, Zoe managed to keep it all these years. I never knew she had it until she brought it out the other night after dinner. You were upstairs rocking Grace, and Zoe said she thought it was time to give it to me."

The single-carat diamond nestling within five white gold prongs winked up at her. "It's beautiful," Robin finally managed to whisper.

"Will you wear it?"

She nodded. "I'd be honored to."

He slid it onto her finger. "We'll get it sized if we need to."

"It's so lovely, Toby." A sob escaped. "I can't believe this is happening."

"It's happening all right. You know what else is happening?"

"What?"

Taking her by the hand, he led her back up to the house's yard to a clear patch of snow. "Now fall backward."

She grinned. "A snow angel?"

Still holding hands, they fell back together and moved their arms and legs in jumping-jack motions. Robin giggled the entire time. She simply couldn't help it.

When they were finished, Toby helped her up so they wouldn't mess up the angels.

She turned to see the design and it brought another lump to her throat. "Hand in hand," she whispered.

"What's that?" Toby asked.

"The snow angels. They're holding hands."

His fingers were still entwined with hers and he lifted her hand to his lips. "It's symbolic. I want to hold your hand forever as we do life. Till death do us part."

"I look forward to doing life with you," Robin told him with a teary-eyed smile.

He slipped his arms around her and held her. Her head fit perfectly under his chin and he kissed the top of her head. "Merry Christmas, Robin."

"Merry Christmas, Toby."

* * * * *

If you enjoyed this story, look for the other books in the Wrangler's Corner series by Lynette Eason:

Dear Reader,

Thank you for once again journeying with me to Wrangler's Corner. I loved Toby from the moment I met him in *Protecting Her Daughter*. I had no idea he would make such a big deal out of having his own story—and his own woman—but he did.

It was a pleasure to see him come to life and learn to love. Neither he nor Robin had an easy childhood, but they rose above it and became two people who appreciated having a happily-ever-after so much more because of it.

I hope that if you're going through any struggles or difficulties, you allow it to make you stronger. Keep pressing on because soon you'll find yourself on the other side of it.

Again, I hope you enjoyed the story. Feel free to let me know at facebook.com/lynette.eason or visit my website at lynetteeason.com to sign up for my newsletter and stay in touch.

God bless,
Lynette

SPECIAL EXCERPT FROM

Love Inspired.
SUSPENSE

*With a price on his witness's head,
US marshal Jonathan Mast can think of only
one place to hide Celeste Alexander—in the
Amish community he left behind. But will this trip
home save their lives…and convince them that a
Plain life together is worth fighting for?*

Read on for a sneak preview of
Amish Hideout *by Maggie K. Black,
the exciting beginning to the Amish Witness Protection
miniseries, available January 2019
from Love Inspired Suspense!*

Time was running out for Celeste Alexander. Her fingers
flew over the keyboard, knowing each keystroke could be
her last before US marshal Jonathan Mast arrived to escort
her to her new life in the witness protection program.

"You gave her a laptop?" US marshal Stacy Preston
demanded. "Please tell me you didn't let her go online."

"Of course not! She had a basic tablet, with the internet
capability disabled." US marshal Karl Adams shot back
even before Stacy had finished her sentence.

The battery died. She groaned. Well, that was that.

"You guys mind if I go upstairs and get my charging
cable?"

LISEXP1218

The room went black. Then she heard the distant sound of gunfire erupting outside.

"Get Celeste away from the windows!" Karl shouted. "I'll cover the front."

What was happening? She felt Stacy's strong hand on her arm pulling her out of her chair.

"Come on!" Stacy shouted. "We have to hurry—"

Her voice was swallowed up in the sound of an explosion, expanding and roaring around them, shattering the windows, tossing Celeste backward and engulfing the living room in smoke. Celeste hit the floor, rolled and hit a door frame. She crawled through it, trying to get away from the smoke billowing behind her.

Suddenly a strong hand grabbed her out of the darkness, taking her by the arm and pulling her up to her feet so sharply she stumbled backward into a small room. The door closed behind them. She opened her mouth to scream, but a second hand clamped over her mouth. A flashlight flickered on and she looked up through the smoky haze, past worn blue jeans and a leather jacket, to see the strong lines of a firm jaw trimmed with a black beard, a straight nose and serious eyes staring into hers.

"Celeste Alexander?" He flashed a badge. "I'm Marshal Jonathan Mast. Stay close. I'll keep you safe."

Don't miss
Amish Hideout by Maggie K. Black,
available January 2019 wherever
Love Inspired® Suspense books and ebooks are sold.

www.LoveInspired.com

LISEXP1218